'No!'

It took all of Sasha's strength to push away from him, her eyes dark with turmoil, with desire. 'No, I can't!'

The taut lines of Rex's face conveyed desire as real as her own, desire and an almost hurt bewilderment, and now she saw an ugly emotion cut across his mouth.

'I'm sorry,' he breathed in a hard, ragged tone. 'I hadn't realised how repulsive it must be for you—being kissed by a cripple.'

Dear Reader

As Easter approaches, Mills & Boon are delighted to present you with an exciting selection of sixteen new titles. Why not take a trip to our Euromance locations—Switzerland or western Crete, where romance is celebrated in great style! Or maybe you'd care to dip into the story of a family feud or a rekindled love affair? Whatever tickles your fancy, you can always count on love being in the air with Mills & Boon!

The Editor

Elizabeth Power was born in Bristol where she lives with her husband in a three-hundred-year-old cottage. A keen reader, as a teenager she had already made up her mind to be a novelist, although it wasn't until around thirty that she took up writing seriously. An animal lover, with a strong leaning towards vegetarianism, her interests include organic vegetable gardening, regular exercise, listening to music, fashion and ministering to the demands of her adopted, generously proportioned cat!

Recent titles by the same author:

CLOSE CAPTIVITY

STRAW ON THE WIND

BY

ELIZABETH POWER

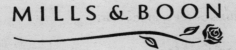

MILLS & BOON LIMITED
ETON HOUSE, 18-24 PARADISE ROAD
RICHMOND, SURREY TW9 1SR

*First published in Great Britain 1994
by Mills & Boon Limited*

© Elizabeth Power 1994

*Australian copyright 1994
Philippine copyright 1994
This edition 1994*

ISBN 0 263 78453 3

*Set in Times Roman 10½ on 12 pt.
01-9404-53166 C*

Made and printed in Great Britain

CHAPTER ONE

THE balloon was descending too quickly!

Sasha's fingers tightened on the edge of the basket until her knuckles showed white, her gaze torn from the stricken features of the young man at the burner— trying desperately to retain some height—to the green and gold fields and the looming grey gables of the manor house with whose towering chimneys they seemed suddenly to be in danger of colliding.

Was this her fate, then? she wondered, feeling sick, her face ashen against her shoulder-length black hair. To fall out of the sky on a summer's evening some- where over Essex? Or was it Suffolk? She wasn't sure how far they had drifted.

'Oh, Gavin! *Do* something!'

Fear turned her eyes to dark sapphire as she looked up into the yawning, striped fabric, her companion's snapped, 'Don't you think I'm *trying*?' unheard as snippets of her twenty-six years seemed to flash, like fragments of an edited film, before her eyes.

Growing up in New York. Her school and her college. Her parents' divorce. Meeting Ben. It was only for mere moments, but her mind relived it all, from her first date with the gentle, bearded young art teacher to that earth-shattering telephone call eighteen months ago that had killed the quiet complacency of her life; the months of anguish and bitterness that had finally driven her here to England to try and escape the loneliness, the memories, the guilt...

'We might do it, Sasha! I levelled off too late, but we might just get away with it!'

Gavin's voice shook her back to the present danger. His teeth were clenched, his face red beneath the sandy hair. Breath held, hardly daring to hope, she watched as a bright burst of flame sent another surge of hot air into the colourful fabric above them.

It held them, reducing the speed of their descent, the evening breeze taking them low over the house. But it wasn't enough, and, only half aware, Sasha noticed the marquee in the rambling grounds beyond the trees, the people—some looking up now—all elegantly dressed. But they were going to come down right through the middle of them if they didn't watch out!

She shot a terrified look at her companion. Felt another blast of heat from the burner. But it was too late for them to miss the trees.

The basket rocked violently as it struck the uppermost branches, wood splintering and cracking as the balloon dragged them relentlessly towards the marquee.

She heard herself scream, heard people shouting. Then she was being thrown, pain stabbing her left shoulder as she struck solidity beneath her, hearing those voices now through a blinding, swirling haze.

'Oh, look what they've done! They've ruined everything!' A female voice drifted down to her, high-pitched and petulant. 'And look what they've done to the marquee!'

'How the devil did they manage...? No, don't touch her!' It was a man's voice this time, deep, laced with authority. 'Before anyone attempts to move her, we'd better make sure she hasn't suffered any serious damage.'

'The poor dear.' A female voice again, but more mature than the first, kinder and with some sort of accent. 'She's out cold.'

No, I'm not! Though the words formed in her brain, she couldn't drag a sound past her lips, half alive to the scent of newly mown grass, to the sounds of chaos. Help me. Help me, please! Shivering, she heard that decisive masculine voice issuing instructions again— the voice of a man who could make things happen— and, as though someone had known, she felt something warm suddenly covering her. As she teetered on the brink of some gaping chasm, her nostrils livened to some other scent, something fresh and pleasant and elusive. For a few anxious moments she thought of Gavin—wondered if he'd made it. And then she was tumbling again, down and down into that dark abyss.

Someone must have carried her inside, she realised when she came to, because she was lying on a bed, gazing up at a high ceiling, and there were voices somewhere in the elegant room.

'I don't know how you're managing to take it so well. I know it was an accident and I do feel sorry for her, but I can't help feeling annoyed. And after all the weeks of planning I'm sure Rex can't be very amused.'

Sasha turned to make out the owner of that petulant remark, a petite young woman—younger than herself—with short blonde hair, standing by the leaded window, the soft rustle of her clothes whispering of chic extravagance as she turned away from the slim, older woman by her side.

'For heaven's sake, Lorraine.' It was that accented voice again—the one she had heard before. 'I know he's prone to moods these days. But good gracious! If a thing like this could get the better of his temper I'd——' The woman broke off, suddenly realising that Sasha was conscious.

'Are you all right, dear? Are you in any pain?' Gentle features smiled concern as the woman came over to her, elegant, strong-boned features softened by greying hair.

'I—I think I'm OK.' Sasha winced as the sudden lift of a hand to her temple revealed otherwise. 'It's...just my shoulder.' Frowning, she strove to recall exactly what had happened, her gaze going back to the long window and out to the wide sweep of lawn.

'Gavin!' Remembering, swiftly she sat up, pain expressing itself in the cornflower-blue of her eyes. 'Gavin...is he...?'

'Perfectly all right,' the older woman reassured in that accent, which was Scots, Sasha comprehended absently, but polished, very refined, like the woman herself. 'He's just across the hall, having treatment for a few cuts and grazes. He'll be all right. So will you, although you passed out for a few minutes, so I think it would be best—just to be on the safe side— if you let someone run you to the hospital.'

Hospital. The place where you waited and waited only to find yourself at the end with nothing. No hopes. No future. Just shattered dreams.

'No!' Quickly she swung her legs over the edge of the bed, panic rising inside of her. 'Oh, gee!' She groaned into her cupped hands, sick with faintness, staring down at the soft denim of her shirt. Beneath it, she realised, someone had loosened her jeans.

'You see, I'm right, dear. The hospital will know what to look for. Lorraine, go and ask Clem to get the car——'

'No!' Panic made her sound unduly sharp, but she couldn't face one of those places again. She couldn't! Wasn't the whole idea of coming to England to forget? 'No, really I'm all right,' she elucidated by way of an apology, but the younger woman clearly wasn't accepting it.

'My aunt's only thinking of what's best for you. Sometimes with concussion serious developments can follow. You could have compression—and that could be fatal.'

'Gee, thanks,' Sasha breathed, looking up, the soft oval of her face pale and lacking make-up in contrast to the pure cosmetic beauty of the other girl's. Lorraine whoever-she-was was a real bundle of fun.

'My niece always was over-imaginative,' her aunt expressed wryly.

'Well, it's true!' was the swift retort. 'Still, if she won't listen to us, perhaps Rex can make her see sense. You know how persuasive he can be, Aunt Sheila, particularly when he's worked up about something. He'll only have to——'

'Lorraine!'

A silencing voice drew everyone's attention to the sheer presence of the man in the doorway. He was impressively built, his white shirt, silver tie and dark trousers bore the stamp of impeccable style, his black hair, parted on the side, emphasising stupendously good looks, and yet there was authority, Sasha noted, in that strongly chiselled face. He was in his early thirties, and maturity had marked that nose and jaw with a forceful arrogance, firming the otherwise sensual line of his mouth with command. A command Sasha had recognised even when she'd been lying semi-conscious on the grass, and which now seemed only to be strengthened by the confines of the wheelchair which bound him.

'It's all right, Mother. Why don't you take my little cousin back outside?'

It was a subtle command and one that was complied with without argument, leaving Sasha feeling oddly vulnerable, suddenly finding herself alone with the man.

'What's your name?' He was manoeuvring his chair into the room with a dexterity long-born of practice, his hands on the wheels, Sasha noticed, lean and tapering, backed by a feathering of dark hair extending down from his wrists.

'Sasha Morgan.'

His lips moved in what could scarcely be termed a smile. 'American?'

She nodded.

'Rex Templeton,' he said.

The hand he offered was cool and impersonal. So this was *the* Rex who was so angry because they'd spoilt his precious garden party! she fumed, quickly retrieving her fingers from the confident clasp of his.

'How do you feel?'

Do you really care? She had to bite her tongue to stop herself saying it. 'I'll live,' she uttered non-chalantly. She didn't want someone who was obviously more concerned about his party than he was about her and Gavin to know that she was in any pain. 'And I'm really sorry about the marquee.' She could see it clearly now that she was sitting up properly; see and hear people scurrying around, rectifying the chaos they had caused with the balloon. Which meant that this room she was occupying was on the ground floor, it dawned upon her then, a room utilised as a bedroom for someone who couldn't get upstairs. It was clearly a man's room too, from the practicality of the dark, natural wood to the no-nonsense statement of the softer furnishings that picked up the subtle tones and style of early Georgian décor. A door leading off would contain a purpose-built *en suite* bathroom, Sasha decided, suddenly feeling awkward, sitting there on his bed.

'Don't let it worry you.' His tone was casually dismissive, his smile almost perfunctory. 'May I?' He reached over and picked up a jacket that was lying on the bed with a waft of pleasingly subtle cologne. That scent she had smelt outside. So it was his jacket she'd felt around her! The thought was strangely discomfiting as she watched him place it casually over his knee. 'I think you should be thanking your lucky stars that you and your boyfriend were let off so lightly. The pair of you could have been killed out there.'

'Yes, I realise that.' Shuddering, she was about to tell him that Gavin Chase wasn't her boyfriend; that she'd only met him the day before when she'd booked a trip in his balloon. But it wasn't important. And she doubted if Rex Templeton would be interested anyway. And as he turned his interest momentarily towards something outside she grabbed the opportunity to study him fully.

He was really, devastatingly handsome, the harsh lines of his features in no way appeased by the raven sleekness of his hair. He had magnetism, unquestionably, way beyond the purely physical, though his shoulders were broad, the tapering lines of his body suggesting a hard, lean strength—despite his disability—beneath the elegant cut of his clothes.

'Do you often make a point of gatecrashing other people's parties in that rather perilous fashion?'

She'd been wondering how such an attractive man had come to be so cruelly handicapped, but eyes that were slaty grey turned, mocking her unguarded interest in him, and, uncomfortably, she swallowed, still bristling from his remark.

'I said I was sorry.' He didn't *look* annoyed, but instinct told her that Rex Templeton would be very adept at keeping his emotions well-hidden, the thought of him simmering beneath that cool façade prompting her tartly to go on, 'I'm sure Gavin is, too. If you can't be understanding enough to realise that it *was* an accident——'

'Hey! Hold on a minute! Are you always this defensive?' he said in hard reproach as he sat back, looking at her from over the top of his clasped hands. She could feel those grey eyes raking criticisingly over her, wise to the angry colour infiltrating what Ben used to call her 'country-girl complexion', and she ran a hand through her dishevelled hair, suddenly conscious of what a mess she must look. 'Aren't you rather taking it on yourself in assuming what I might be thinking?'

He was right, she thought. He hadn't actually done or said anything to warrant such aggression from her and with a sheepish little grimace she said, 'I'm sorry. It's just that I heard your... cousin saying that you'd been planning this party for weeks...'

'Ah, Lorraine.' For a moment his eyes were shielded by intensely dark eyelashes, and there was a curiously indulgent twist to his mouth. 'Always the divine hostess to my needs. But apologies aren't necessary— certainly not to me. If you must express needless contrition, save it for my mother. It was her sixtieth the two of you invaded—and nothing to do with Lorraine.'

'I'm sorry...'

'Oh, don't worry.' He pulled a wry face at the genuine regret Sasha knew showed in hers. 'I'm sure she'll forgive you for it. Probably far more than she will if you ignore her well-meaning advice to let someone drive you to the hospital.'

'No!' Of course, that was why he had come in, to deal with her obstinacy over doing the sensible thing. And now she felt his gaze lance across her, down to her fingers curling tensely into the dark maroon of the duvet.

'You've been concussed,' he said.

'I passed out,' she stated with a defiant lift of her chin.

'Yes! Probably from contact with a tent pole.'

'From fright,' she amended argumentatively, and saw a sceptical eyebrow rise.

'Even so...don't you think it would be a good idea to make doubly sure——?'

'No!' She made to push herself up and winced as her bruised shoulder protested, and she flopped back with a painful groan on to the bed.

'Take it easy.' For the first time she saw a flicker of something nearing compassion in his eyes. 'Where are you staying?' he pressed in level tones then.

'That depends.' Absently, she secured her hair behind one ear, guessing that Gavin must have informed him she was there on vacation.

'On what?'

On a lot of things, she thought. Like how the money stretches, because she had planned over a month's stay around London and Constable country, and already her first week here had eaten considerably into her budget. But she said only, 'On how lucky I am with getting a site for the tent or whether I have to book into a hotel. At the moment I'm camping—about three or four miles from here, I guess.'

'What . . . *alone*?' He was frowning down at her as though she were mad, and she wondered if Gavin had supplied him with that information, too.

'Sure. Why not?' she challenged.

That slaty gaze made a cursory yet unsettling appraisal of her slender figure. 'Isn't that rather an unwise pastime for a young woman on her own?'

Sasha took a deep breath. A year ago she might have agreed with him, but a lot had changed since then. She had learned nothing if not that life was cheap, she thought bitterly, pain of an emotional kind knitting her fine brows, making her say quickly—carelessly, 'Is it?'

His expression was hard but unreadable. 'I wouldn't want a daughter—or any female relative of mine for that matter—to do it,' he expressed. And more drily, 'But then you seem to indulge in rather hazardous pursuits, don't you?'

Like crashing into his beautiful grounds in a balloon! Impetuously, for a moment, she wondered if he resented the fact that she and Gavin at least had the choice, while he was imprisoned in that chair, but that deep voice was cutting across her thoughts.

'That boyfriend of yours told me a few things about you—plus the fact that he's a local lad himself. He also said that you're here for five or six weeks, and if you're camping you obviously didn't fly over here to stay with him. In which case I can only assume that you haven't known him that long, so what is an attractive young woman doing holidaying alone so far from home? In my experience most women aren't usually that adventurous.'

And he would have had a lot of that, she accepted, startled by how acutely aware she was herself of that lethal magnetism.

Forgetting her shoulder, she shrugged. 'Well, here's one who is.'

'And clearly paying for it,' he grimaced, obviously noting that scarcely discernible wince. 'But you haven't answered my question.'

No, she hadn't, had she? she thought, catching her breath as the too familiar anguish welled up inside, like salt water flowing into a wound that refused to heal. It was too painful and personal to her—the reason why she'd needed to get away from New York; too personal to share with a cold-blooded middle-class Englishman like Rex Templeton. 'My grandmother came from this part of the world,' she explained as steadily as she was able. 'I also paint—I'm a children's illustrator. Consequently, the chance to see not only the place where my grandmother's family came from but also where John Constable—my favourite artist—lived and worked was too tempting to resist.'

He seemed satisfied with that, swinging his chair away, turning as he reached the leaded window. 'Well, Sasha Morgan...' A shaft of evening sunlight played across his tilted head, brushing the gleaming sable with fire. 'If you won't accept any medical supervision, then I must insist that you stay here—at least for tonight. You can't possibly go roughing it in a tent when it obviously hurts even to move. Apart from which, you injured yourself on my property—therefore I can't help feeling some responsibility for you—more, I think than you're evidently showing for yourself.'

'I *am* twenty-six!' Sasha threw at him, needled, and, ignoring the pain in her shoulder, got to her feet, fastening the waistband of her jeans.

'So mature.' Mockery touched his lips, and his gaze fell to her hands, making her blush scarlet from how personal he had made the action seem.

'Yes. And I've really no intention of imposing on your hospitality any further,' she breathed, piqued by his lordly attitude, but even more by that unsettling sensual arrogance as she made more than a necessary show of pulling down her shirt. But then Gavin came in, wearing various dressings and a look of pure relief to see her on her feet, his, 'Thank goodness you're all right!' somewhat premature as she swayed a little unsteadily, and, for her own sake, sank down again on to the bed.

'We'll be keeping Sasha here tonight,' she heard Rex Templeton conveying decisively over the soft protest of the chair as he manoeuvred it swiftly towards the door. And with a challenging glance at her over his shoulder, 'I'll see that there's a room prepared for her upstairs,' was his pre-emptory statement, killing any opposition stone-dead.

So he had taken the decision away from her, she realised, cursing her weakness in feeling faint right at that moment, although, contrarily, then—and much later, during the course of the evening—she was glad he had.

She'd hardly have been up to scrambling about in a field, she thought wryly when, stiff and fatigued, she was soaking in the huge green marble corner bath adjacent to the luxurious four-poster bedroom they had given her. And Gavin had seemed more than pleased that the Templetons had asked her to stay.

'Phew!' He had whistled approvingly, barely before their host had left them in that downstairs room. 'What a place this is!' He'd been so impressed he'd virtually ignored her anxious query as to how he was. 'Do you know how rich that guy is? What he's worth?' he'd enthused, looking around at the tastefully expensive furnishings, and his questions had been laced with unmistakable awe. 'He owns one of the biggest electronic companies this side of the Atlantic—not to mention all the money he made out of that land he sold some years back for that golf course we came over. How on earth did you manage to wangle it? Getting a passport on to Templeton territory? Not that I'm jealous!' he'd laughed. 'But I wouldn't mind changing places with that guy any day of the week!'

Which he could hardly have meant! she thought. Having to spend every day in a wheelchair. And at twenty-five, as a sales executive working in London, Gavin's own prospects had to be very good. Nevertheless, she'd found herself unable to restrain her curiosity about Rex Templeton—what it was that prevented him from walking—and she recalled Gavin's brief explanation when she had asked.

'A motor accident. Not his fault—the other chap's—and *he* got off without a scratch. It was two years ago, I think—it was in all the papers. I think it's doubtful, though, that he'll ever walk again.'

Commiserating, she'd wanted to know more about the man personally, inexplicably curious, but Gavin had changed the subject, making her promise to keep in touch with him—insisting on it before leaving to join his back-up team who had been following the balloon by road.

Now, though, wallowing in the creamy lather, it was Rex Templeton, and not Gavin Chase, to whom her thoughts kept straying, still seeing those incredibly handsome features, that dark, forceful presence—until, realising it, annoyed with herself, she thrust her preoccupation with him to the back of her mind.

He might be a man, and a very attractive one, but she'd be out of his house tomorrow and he'd be part of the past. Apart from which, she didn't want involvements—no matter how dynamic a man might be—she couldn't risk it. Loving people hurt. And she couldn't stand the agony of that ever again. She'd loved Ben and he'd left her. A rare heart disease, they had said. But what they didn't know was that he might have been alive today if it hadn't been for her.

CHAPTER TWO

SASHA felt considerably better—both mentally and physically—the following morning, particularly after the nourishing breakfast which Sheila Templeton had sent up to her room. Her clothes had been freshly laundered, too, she noticed gratefully, taking them into the bathroom, relieved to see, from the mirror above the basin, that the colour had returned to her cheeks.

Having black hair, which she liked to wear parted on one side, around her face, and with the natural ebony of her brows and lashes, there was always the danger of looking too washed-out when she wasn't well, she thought with a grimace, remembering how she'd looked after the accident yesterday and taking care to avoid putting any unnecessary strain on her bruised shoulder as she showered and dressed and then made her way downstairs.

All last night's guests had left, she remembered Sheila telling her earlier, and, knowing a strange relief that she wouldn't be meeting Lorraine, Sasha paused to admire the grandeur of the imposing oak-panelled hall, taking in the complementary richness of the furnishings, the majestic stone fireplace, and, overhead, the gnarled and ancient beams.

'It's eighteenth century, if you're wondering.'

Sasha pivoted to meet Rex Templeton's startling presence, the strong contours of his face softened by the lazy twist of a smile.

'You made me jump,' she breathed, her hand going to her chest, because she hadn't heard the chair approaching. Neither had she seen him since he'd left her in that room last night, the clean-cut, tailored elegance of the man taking her breath away.

'I'm sorry.' Unwittingly her senses sharpened to the resonance of his voice, to that aura of dark strength about him that was disturbingly male. 'As I said, it's eighteenth century. One of my forefathers had it built for his bride and it's been in my family ever since. My father passed it on to me when he died seven years ago, along with more land than I could cope with and a devil of a maintenance liability!' He laughed, his teeth showing strong and white against his olive skin. 'Believe me, being the owner of a stately home—albeit a small one—isn't always the enviable proposition some people might think.'

Sasha felt her cheeks burning, wondering for one awkward moment if he had overhead the things Gavin had been saying the previous night.

'But let's talk about you.' He might not have overheard, but she could feel those steely eyes upon her, keen and sharply perceptive. 'I hear you've managed to convince my mother that you're fit enough to leave.' His assessing glance over her denim-clothed figure told her he'd be somewhat harder to convince.

'It's only a bruised shoulder,' she uttered dismissively, 'but apart from that I'm fine. Will it be all right if I call a cab?'

'To take you to your tent?' There was an edge of disparagement in his voice, needling her as she remembered just what he thought of her carefree style of living, but he said only, 'I'm going into London this morning. I can give you a lift to save you the trouble. I'll be leaving in fifteen minutes if you can be ready by then.'

She was. After all, she hadn't exactly been that endowed with luggage when she had dropped in last night, she thought, grimacing at the unintended pun as she belted her pouch-bag around her waist, picked up her camera, which seemed miraculously to be undamaged, and hurried downstairs to the car.

It was a white BMW, long and sleek and expensive, and a surly, middle-aged man in a mariner's cap offered only a brusque good morning to her as he opened the back passenger door.

'Don't be put off by Clem.' Beside them, Rex sent a conspiratorial smile up at the other man. 'What he lacks in conversation, he makes up for in loyalty. It was Clem, incidentally, who carried you in last night.'

'I see,' she murmured, sliding across the seat, but thought, Only because you couldn't, aware that whatever situation Rex Templeton found himself in he would automatically be the leader, in command.

He was easing himself out of his chair with the aid of crutches, and, not wanting to appear to be staring, Sasha made a point of looking away—out at the unexpectedly grey morning—as he swung himself heavily on to the seat beside her.

'What's the matter?' he said roughly. 'Does my crippled state embarrass you? It would seem you weren't so reticent about discussing it with your friend, Gavin, last night.'

He'd *heard*?

Mortified, Sasha sent a startled glance in his direction, and, seeing the bitter twist to his lips, realised he must have heard everything else that Gavin had been saying as well.

'I'm sorry. I didn't... I mean, I had no idea...' She was floundering in a sea of crimson embarrassment. Why hadn't she stopped Gavin from going on like that last night?

Out of the corner of her eye she saw that arrogant jaw lift and above the sound of the chair being folded into the boot heard him take a short, sharp breath.

'Tell me something, Sasha,' he rasped, when the chauffeur was sliding into the driving seat. 'Would *you* change places with me?'

His question had all the cutting power of a serrated knife and imperceptibly she shivered. He was really making her pay for discussing him with the other man, she thought—obviously extremely sensitive, and probably very bitter, about what had happened to him. And who could blame him? she sympathised, weighing all his wealth—his house, this lovely car— against the simple luxury of being able to walk.

'No,' she said truthfully, her gaze fixed on the wiper-blades removing a few drops of rain from the windscreen.

'Hear that, Clem? At least she's honest!' he uttered with a harsh, humourless laugh that made Sasha recoil with unease.

If you want to make me feel bad about it, you've succeeded! she felt like retorting hotly, objecting to being used as a source of cynical amusement between him and his surly chauffeur as they started down the long gravelled drive.

At the gates they had to wait for a tractor to grumble noisily past before pulling out, giving Sasha time to digest the words on the ornate black sign on one of the pillars. 'The Halt'.

'A rather ironical prophecy, don't you think?'

She hadn't even realised how absorbed her interest was until that deep voice grazed across her thoughts, and she tensed, realising from the taut line of his mouth that he was still referring to his immobility. But then with another curt laugh he said, 'Since you obviously know everything about me, then, tell me something about Sasha Morgan. You said you're a children's illustrator back there in the States? What exactly does that entail?'

Glad that he had brought the conversation round to a more comfortable topic, Sasha let out a discreet sigh of relief. 'It means I paint pictures to accompany children's stories—sometimes in collaboration with the author, sometimes after the manuscripts have already been supplied. I've also written a little myself—several small books that I've also supplied illustrations for. Only small-time,' she went on to add hastily, seeing the way his mouth quirked, not wanting him to be impressed when really there was nothing to be impressed about. 'It's only the type of thing you might pick up for kiddies in your supermarkets.' But she didn't add that the little books she had wanted to continue writing herself had dried up since Ben had died; that the last one had been rejected, her literary inspiration, if not her artistic one, sadly curtailed. 'I've also done some nature studies for calendars, greetings cards, that sort of thing.'

Rex's smile was cool but genuine. 'Sounds interesting,' he remarked.

'It is.' Her own smile conveyed her satisfaction in the job she loved. 'It also pays the rent.'

'Do you live alone?'

He could hardly be interested, she thought. In a few minutes he'd be dropping her off, probably relieved to get rid of her. But she answered, 'Yes. Yes, I do,' and felt the sudden hard penetration of his glance.

Had he detected the deliberate carelessness in her voice? The emotion she was trying hard not to convey?

'Mom lives just outside New York—Dad in New England,' she continued quickly, and with a pull of her lips, 'Both with different spouses. I lived with my mother after she and Dad divorced about ten years ago and when she married again she followed Dad's example and moved out of town. I could have gone with her but I chose to stay.' Because then there had been someone to stay for, she thought with a swift, silent catch of her breath, suddenly feeling a fool for gabbling on and telling Rex Templeton so much—a virtual stranger, someone she would probably never see again when he let her out of his car.

'Is that it? Over there?'

The brusque voice of Clem Baldwin cut sharply across her thoughts.

'Yes,' she said, looking towards the red-brick farmhouse at which he was pointing, and the adjoining field where a pyramid of blue canvas was peeping above the hedge.

'Well, well. You do believe in living dangerously, don't you?' Rex commented drily as the BMW drew up alongside her battered blue Mini.

'Thanks,' she retorted, seeing the amusement in his eyes. 'But funds didn't exactly run to the cost of anything better.'

He looked at her aghast. 'You mean you bought it?'

'Well, it was cheaper than hiring one,' she assured him, indignant over his ridiculing her little car, 'and, apart from a dodgy hand-brake I managed to get sorted out, it goes. Anyway, thanks for everything...' She was having difficulty getting out because the door was stiff, and she caught her breath from his startling proximity as he suddenly leaned across her, pushing it open with comparative ease.

'What are you going to do now?' He almost sounded as though he cared.

'What I came here to do. *Paint*,' she stressed, stepping out into the drizzle. She didn't intend a hectic sightseeing trip of the country. She had done that before when her father had decided it would be a good way for her to get to know her new stepmother some years ago and it had been a good trip, but this time she just wanted to lose herself in the English countryside. 'I guess I'll stay around here for a few weeks and if that heap of a wreck...' with a deliberate reminder of what he thought about her Mini, she jerked her chin towards it '...manages to get me to a dealer, I'll trade it in——'

Suddenly she stopped short, looking puzzled at the little car. Something was wrong. Oh, God, please...

'What is it?' Rex's voice came low and clipped through the open door.

'I don't know. The window's open. I didn't leave it open. At least I don't think I did,' she mused worriedly, clutching the top of the BMW's door to support her suddenly weak legs.

'You don't *think* you did?' Those deep tones sounded rather impatient with her now.

'I *know* I didn't,' she said adamantly, moving away. She wouldn't have. She was as security-conscious as any guard at Fort Knox!

Even so, before she opened the car door she could see the trailing wires where the radio had been. A sweater, her sunglasses and the map she had left folded on the back seat were missing too.

'What sort of people would do a thing like this?' she groaned, dismayed, going round to the boot. 'Oh, no!'

It lifted instantly without her even having to use her key, the paintwork scratched and buckled where the lock had been forced. 'My passport! My bag with my passport! Traveller's cheques! Everything! They've taken that!' Plus most of her camping equipment that had been locked away for safe keeping, she realised, rummaging chaotically through what little was left. 'My sketches!' With a small cry she clutched the sketchpad, which was mercifully still there, to her breast as though it were a wounded infant, too relieved to take any consolation then from the fact that the thieves had at least also left her her clothes. 'They've taken practically everything—except my sketches and my case,' she groaned, feeling the cold splashes of rain on her cheeks, dampening her hair, unaware that the BMW had reversed, parallel with her, until a commanding voice instructed,

'Get back in the car.'

Slamming down the boot of the Mini, blindly she complied, near to tears as she stepped back into the cushioning warmth of the BMW.

'What am I going to do now?' Anxiously, she murmured her desolate thoughts aloud.

'Well, first we let the police know. Report the loss of your passport—and any other important documents you've had taken. What on earth possessed you to leave a thing like your passport in the car?' he breathed incredulously, lifting the phone between the two front seats, stabbing out a number, calmly, coolly, in control.

'It *was* in the boot,' Sasha stressed. 'I thought it would be safer to leave everything there than carrying it all around with me while I went up in that balloon. Anyway, I didn't realise I'd be gone all night——'

'Police?' He cut across her indignant little speech, those incredibly long lashes lowered as he gave his name and address and explained what had happened. 'Yes, she's a guest of mine,' he said, and now that inscrutable grey gaze roved reflectively over her damp hair, her pale, worried features, probably considering her a fool. 'Could you send someone over right away?'

Which, of course, they would—for him, Sasha thought, wishing he could have driven off before he'd discovered this further dilemma she was facing.

'You'd better collect what's left of your things and come back to the house,' he was stating decisively. 'Leave the Mini. I'll send someone else to pick it up. You're in no fit state to drive. Clem?' Just a tilt of his head and the chauffeur was getting out to retrieve her suitcase, but before Sasha could protest, already feeling uncomfortably indebted to the man sitting beside her, he was making another call.

'I'll be later than I intended,' he informed whoever had been expecting him. Probably his office, she guessed, watching the stalwart Clem wielding her case easily with one hand, while deciding—just as she had probably, she thought, seeing him closing the boot—that what remained wasn't worth taking.

'Look, you don't have to do this,' she protested to Rex when Clem was back in the driving seat, pulling away. 'I've put you to enough trouble already.' She looked apologetically at him, an aloof, impeccable stranger whose day she was upsetting because she'd had her passport stolen, a careless American whom he had allowed to stay overnight at his home because she had injured herself, and towards whom he felt some measure of responsibility.

'What am I supposed to do? Throw you back into the bushes?' Mockery gleamed for a moment in the slaty grey of his eyes. 'I take it you've got the receipts for those traveller's cheques?'

Then it hit her—the total seriousness of her predicament. 'Yes. No. What I mean is—I knew I wouldn't have a definite base so I didn't want to risk bringing them because of the merest chance that something like this might happen. They're at home,' she told him lamely.

'But you've got a note of the numbers.'

It wasn't even a question—that was how sure he was that she would have—her half timorous, 'No,' producing a look that told her he thought her a total imbecile.

Which was how she was beginning to feel, she thought, as he asked crisply, 'Do you have any other money?'

'Some,' she uttered, glancing down at her pouch-bag, but hardly enough to see her through. And now she was going to have to telephone her mother, drag her all the way to the apartment to get those receipts, she realised hopelessly, before she could even begin to sort things out with the bank.

'You're in one hell of a mess, lady.' That broad chest expanded with impatience and she turned away, staring at the damp, flitting countryside so that she couldn't see the hard censure in his profile. Then after a few moments she heard him say, 'May I?'

He was reaching for the sketchpad that was on the seat between them, and she nodded, feeling a curious tightening in her stomach. Her problems weren't getting to him as they were to her, she thought, apprehensively aware of him turning the paper leaves, assessing her watercolour flowers, plants and insects with a lazy, almost indifferent air. He was right, though. She'd got herself into a real mess, and through no one's fault but her own. Nor did it make her feel any better when, on reaching the Halt, Rex simply handed back her sketches without comment—clearly as unimpressed with them as he was with her, she thought dejectedly as he said, 'Go on inside. I'll be with you in a few minutes.'

And that was all it took for the police to arrive and make her feel doubly careless, with their rather condescending questions. Which wouldn't have been so bad, she thought, if they hadn't shown such amazing deference to Rex, so that sitting there among the green and apricot tones of the elegant drawing-room, watching Sheila Templeton pour tea, Sasha found herself wishing she were anywhere but there, imposing on her hostess's kind hospitality.

'Why don't you phone your mother, dear?' the woman suggested when the police had left. She was collecting up the fine china cups with a soft ringing sound as she put each one on the tray.

'New York?' Sasha felt the need to remind her, not wishing to sink further into Rex Templeton's debt. She wasn't even sure she had enough money to recompense them for the call.

'Do it.' In the high-ceilinged room, Rex's tone invited no argument, and gratefully Sasha hurried to the phone on the antique polished table beside the sofa, sighing her frustration when only a monotonous ringing tone answered her anxious attempt.

'She must be out.' It was to Rex that she turned her dark, desolate gaze rather than his mother. 'There's no reply,' she uttered disconsolately.

'Then try again—and keep trying until there is,' he sanctioned firmly as he pushed back an immaculate shirt-cuff to glance at his watch. 'I have to go.' With a cool deftness he had put the wheelchair into motion. 'Keep her here until I get back,' he instructed his mother. 'I shan't be too late this evening.' And then, as he drew level with Sasha who had subsided back on to the sofa, 'Don't worry.' There was an edge of understanding in his voice, solicitude in that strong countenance. 'We'll sort it out,' he promised.

After he had gone, though, she felt decidedly alone, particularly when further attempts to reach her mother continued to prove futile. She rang the American embassy to report the theft of her passport. Then some time during the afternoon a young male member of the Templeton staff came in to inform her that when the thieves had ripped the radio out of her car they had broken some of the wires controlling the electrics and that on Mr Templeton's instructions he had taken it to the garage for repairs.

So now she not only had no passport and no money, but no car either, she thought despairingly, deciding that things couldn't possibly be any worse. That was until, as the afternoon crept into a muggy evening and another call to New York brought no response, she suddenly remembered her mother telling her that she might be taking a short break while Sasha was in England, and now a cold fear gripped her heart.

'Oh, *no*. Please...' In desperation she was stabbing out the number of her mother's closest neighbour, who, fortunately, was at home, but who then only confirmed her worst fears. Her mother was indeed away. But no, the woman apologised. She didn't have an address where she could be reached.

Dropping the phone back on to its rest, Sasha exhaled a long sigh, her shoulders hunching in despair. What was she supposed to do now? she wondered hectically, just as a deep voice from the doorway drawled, 'Problems?'

Her heart lurched to see Rex, though she failed to see why. He could hardly help her out of this situation, could he? she reasoned, wondering if it was that raw confidence about him that made her so relieved that he was home as she answered, 'More than I anticipated.'

'Your mother's away?'

Of course. He would have gleaned that from the one-sided conversation he had overheard, she realised, giving a hopeless little shrug. 'Not only that, I don't know how long for—and I can't even get in touch!' And to add to everything else she could feel her bruised shoulder really starting to ache now, although that was the least of her worries!

'You've really learnt a hard lesson, haven't you?' he exhaled, wheeling himself in, that note of censure in his voice rubbing like steel wool over Sasha's already frayed nerves.

'If you're going to give me a lecture on responsibility, then save it,' she advised him heatedly. 'I know I've probably been very stupid, and I'm feeling sick enough about it as it is without having to listen to someone else telling me how negligent I've been!'

Now throw me out! she thought, feeling wretched from the hopelessness of her situation, aware of his gaze tugging coolly over her shirt and jeans and back to her natural complexion—bright with flustered colour.

'Sit down,' he commanded softly.

Surprised, she obeyed, disturbed to find herself thinking, in spite of all her problems, how a woman might easily fall prey to the seduction in that deep voice, her throat contracting as he twisted round to push the door closed behind him.

'It hasn't been very comfortable for you in my country so far, has it?' he said, his gaze touching briefly on her painful shoulder, almost as though he knew. 'First that accident—now this. I take it everything was insured?'

'Yes.' At least she could admit to that much!

'So what do you propose to do now?'

She was unaware of how strained she looked, sitting there, putting on a brave face. 'I guess I'll have to go to the embassy,' she said, trying to sound positive. What *did* one do when one was alone in a strange country and had lost everything, including one's passport? Right then, the only course which she could see open to her was to sell the car as soon as it came back from the garage and pay for her ticket home!

'You could stay on here.'

His offer came so startlingly out of the blue that Sasha looked up, dumbfounded. His features, though, were rigid and unsmiling. He was deadly serious! she thought.

'The room you slept in last night isn't being used,' he went on when she was too flabbergasted to answer. 'It would be simple enough for Clem to take your things upstairs, and you'd have a decent roof over your head while you were sorting out the dreadful mess you're in now—no more worries about where to stay—for the rest of your holiday, if you so desire. And it would be far more comfortable than camping,' he finished with a smile. Casually he was massaging the muscles at the back of his neck. 'Well?' he pressed softly, those grey eyes holding hers with disconcerting steadiness, unsettling her, giving her no room to think.

'I don't know. I——' She hesitated, biting her lip, her gaze dropping to the shirt that raised arm had pulled taut across his chest so that she see the dark shading of his body-hair beneath. It was a generous offer, but she couldn't afford such luxurious accommodation as the Halt would provide, because he surely wasn't suggesting she should stay there for nothing— no one was *that* generous! she thought, only her desperate position compelling her to reconsider. 'You mean I could settle with you when I eventually replace my lost cheques?'

A wall-clock chimed, slow and stately, over the fireplace, emphasising the silence—that briefest pause before he answered, 'Cash payment wasn't entirely what I had in mind.'

A fine tension crept along her veins and she looked at him warily. 'Just what exactly *did* you have in mind?'

He hadn't failed to detect that little tremor in her voice—and worse, she realised, her reluctant awareness of him as a man. Sensual mockery played around his lips, though his eyes had taken on the

quality of flint. She could sense, too, the tension in
those fingers that were suddenly gripping his chair as
he said grazingly, 'And what makes you so presump-
tuous as to assume I might even be in a position
to...take advantage of you?'

Sasha swallowed, colouring. Of course, she hadn't
even considered that his life might have been even
more devastated than was first apparent. There would
be emotional scars, too, deep and bitter. Wasn't she
only too aware herself of how cruel life could be?

'I—I didn't mean...' Awkwardly, her sentence tailed
away. Why was she always saying the wrong thing?

'Skip it,' he said curtly, dismissing her blushing
apologies just as his mother came in to tell him that
he was wanted on his private line. And with that he
pushed himself away, telling her to direct Sasha to the
garden room.

Puzzled, therefore, she followed the woman across
the hall into a corridor and a light, airy room where
leaded French windows looked out on to a flagged
patio. A shrub garden lay beyond, stretching away to
the woods and the silent water-meadows of the fertile
valley, misted now by the fine rain.

'This used to be one huge room, but Rex had it
converted into his own personal suite after...well,
after the accident,' Sheila told her hesitantly, indicating towards the open door of an adjacent room.
His bedroom, Sasha realised with a small jolt, recog-
nising the room she had woken up in yesterday, wondering why he had instructed his mother to bring her
here.

'It's lovely,' she appreciated, noting the fully stacked
bookcase that took up practically one wall, the cane

furniture, and the white marble fireplace on the opposite wall beside an alcove, a small, arched recess which, devoid of any ornamentation, oddly lacked the natural ambience and taste of the rest of the room.

'Rex shouldn't be long.'

Sasha smiled her thanks as the other woman went out, running her hand absently along the smooth cane of one of the chairs. With those moss-green rugs and natural-toned furnishings, and that abundance of exotic-looking plants, the room seemed very much an extension of the garden . . .

'Were you criticising or admiring with that artistic eye of yours?'

She had been too engrossed in her surroundings to notice the silent approach of the wheelchair, and pivoted to meet Rex's cool, speculative smile.

'Both,' she admitted, too burdened by the weight of her problems to offer much of one in return, which he must have misinterpreted as nervousness, as he then glanced towards the adjacent room, saying drily, 'Would it make you feel safer to close that door?'

Sasha stayed exactly where she was, flushing from the uncomfortable reminder of her imprudent remark in the drawing-room, but before she could recover herself Rex was carrying on, 'You wanted to know what I'd expect in return for my hospitality. And just to dispel any notion that I offer every distraught young woman I come across a bed in this house . . .' He pointed towards the empty recess beside the fireplace. 'You see this alcove here?'

Trying to shrug off her discomfiture, Sasha moved nearer the fireplace, finding it even harder to shake off her awareness of that hard, compelling masculinity. 'Yes. What does it normally house?'

'Housed,' he corrected, and with a dismissive gesture, 'A statue. Just a small sculpture. I've been wondering what to put in its place. Now I've decided. As you can appreciate, I can't get out into the countryside as easily as I would like, so I would like you to bring the countryside in here to me. I'd like you to paint a fresco in that recess for me—something that would reflect the outdoor aspect of the rest of the room. I'd give you free rein with it, and you could do it at your leisure—whenever you felt like it—so that it wouldn't interfere with any other plans you have while you're here. Do that for me and in exchange I shall give you bed and full board if you want it for the rest of your holiday.'

Sasha viewed him obliquely, her hair like dark silk brushing her shoulder. 'What makes you think I'd be good enough?' she breathed.

That forceful chin tilted to some unseen object behind him. 'Your references,' he said, with the barest glimmer of a smile.

He meant her sketches, she realised, which were still sitting on the hall table. So he had been impressed by them this morning even if he hadn't said so at the time!

'But I...' Still having difficulty taking in his proposition, Sasha moved over to the narrow recess, running her hands over the smooth, finely plastered wall. 'I've never done anything on such a large scale as this before,' she admitted, daunted by the prospect. How could she do justice to those elaborate cornices? Apply her simple watercolour skills to something that would complement the flawless, natural mood of the room?

'What's the problem?' She was aware of his chair moving closer to her, of that subtle, elusive fragrance of his cologne. 'Aren't you up to the challenge?'

'It isn't that,' she returned with an unconscious lift of her chin from the very suggestion of it. But how could she tell him that she found the prospect of sharing the same roof with him more intimidating even than what he was asking her to do? That she had come to this country to be alone?

'What, then?' he pursued, sitting back to look at her. 'From those sketches and paintings I would have thought a nature study would have been right up your street. If we had sprays of something here...' He sat forward, indicating what he meant. 'Grasses or fern perhaps coming down that side—and a splash of something here...in the centre here...' he made a circular movement with his outstretched hand '...perhaps a subtle dove-grey or very pale yellow——'

'Hardly.' She grimaced at his vain suggestion to give the alcove some life. 'Not if you want to see it. It might be recessed, but you still get some light from the window—and it would look colourless when the sun was reflecting off that wall,' she explained, gesturing towards the one adjacent to the hall, 'and at other times it would be lost in shadow. The grass idea is great, but what you need in the centre are small splashes of something bolder, a deep russet or even vermilion, just a touch but strong enough to draw the eye straight to it.'

'Then you'll do it?' He was smiling innocently up at her, but a mischievous glint in his eyes told her that he had purposely fired her enthusiasm with that

ostensible lack of taste, knowing that her artistic pride
wouldn't be able to stop her from putting him straight.

'You did that deliberately, didn't you?' she re-
proved, thwarted by his cleverness, and had her sus-
picions confirmed when she saw that hard mouth
curve in smug triumph.

'Supposing you don't like it?' she suggested
worriedly.

He leaned back in his chair with that cool self-poise.
'Then I'll have it painted over immediately and you
can find some other way to reimburse me,' he smiled,
and in a way that was so blatantly sensual that Sasha
felt her throat contract, her pulse throb in response.

'Well?' His eyes mocked the hectic colour in her
cheeks as he held out his hand. 'Do we have a deal?'

Sasha hesitated for a second, then murmured her
agreement, slipping her hand into his. As before, she
recognised its cool strength, but today those fingers
lingered a little too long around hers, causing a wary
knot of tension in her stomach.

And that had to be an over-reaction, she thought
afterwards—susceptibility caused by shock because
of all that had happened, and because, after all, he
was so glaringly handsome. But if Ben had lived, she
would have been Mrs Benjamin Richards now,
wouldn't she? she thought achingly. And, no matter
how charismatic Rex Templeton was, the simple truth
was, she couldn't allow herself to get that close to any
man again, not after what had happened. There would
never be a repeat of last time. Her guilt would
see to that.

CHAPTER THREE

SASHA started work on the fresco two days later, having spent the previous one sorting out her passport with her embassy, and then, with money provided by Rex, acquiring the necessary materials she needed to begin her task.

Now, with a watercolour medium, diligently she applied the first touches of golden yellow to the plaster, a shrewd skill in the fine brushstrokes that created her first representation of nature, vibrantly aware that Rex would expect nothing less than perfection, that he knew exactly what he wanted. The discussion they had had about composition and colour earlier had told her that.

Two hours into her work, she stood back to survey it, tensing as the creak of the wheelchair in the hall signalled Rex's approach.

'Have you had coffee yet?' he demanded, coming in.

Sasha could only shake her head, rocked by the sheer impact of his masculinity. He had discarded his jacket because of the hot day that had necessitated her opening the French windows earlier, the short-sleeved shirt exposing his strong forearms, while his darkly clad hips were encased by trousers that were impeccably creased. 'I didn't want to stop until I'd finished this rather intricate bit,' she found her voice to say now, daubing fine seeds on an illusion of ripe grasses with her brush.

'And now you have?' He was angling his chair to survey her work with a keen, assessing eye, and nervously Sasha held her breath.

'You...said you wouldn't make any comment until it was completed,' she uttered, tentatively reminding him of the promise he had made to her two days before.

'Of course.' His smile was breath-catching as he swung himself to face her, his unsettling regard making her conscious of how much shapely leg she was showing in her khaki shorts, of the careless daubs of yellow on her green T-shirt. 'I only came to tell you that I had a message from the garage that your car's ready and waiting. I've arranged for someone to go down and pick it up.'

'Oh. Th-thanks. But you didn't have to. I mean...' Why did she always feel like a stammering idiot when he was around? 'What I mean is...I'm not able to pay for it yet,' she finished, abashed, since further unanswered phone calls to New York had only ascertained that her mother was still away, and she was already in his debt through a small loan he'd given her before she'd gone to London yesterday.

'No,' he accepted, totally unperturbed, that warm gaze holding her in sway.

The sun blazing in through the open windows gave a unique opalescence to his eyes, touching on the sleek, two-tone silver of his tie and the finely tailored shirt so that it was an effort to drag her attention back to her painting, utter with a little tremor, 'Well, what do you think?'

'I thought you didn't want criticism.' Against the melodious note of a blackbird in the shrubbery, he sounded almost amused.

Of course. What a fool she must look!

'It's hardly my intention to interrupt the creative flow before it's hardly got going,' he said, and with his gaze straying over her flushed oval face, over the dark sheen of her hair, 'Do I unsettle you that much?'

The brush Sasha was holding nearly slid from her grasp, every nerve quivering from the sensuality behind his question. 'No, of course not,' she lied. And without turning his way, 'Why on earth should you think that?'

'Let's call it experience,' he said.

She ventured a lofty glance at him now. 'And yours stretches far and wide?'

He laughed, his strong face alive, vibrantly male. 'You've really got discriminating ideas about me, haven't you?'

'Have I?' Heart pounding like a bass drum, she wasn't sure how she was keeping her brush steady, somehow still managing to sound convincing when she said, 'I really hadn't given it that much thought.'

'Which really puts me in my place, doesn't it?' he breathed, his smile sardonic, although the creak of that chair moving closer brought a surge of heat washing over her skin with the suspicion that he wasn't ready yet to let this subject go. 'What would you do, I wonder, if I——?'

'Rex... Oh! I'm sorry.' The timely interruption came from a well-dressed middle-aged woman who had stopped in the doorway, the tied red silk of her blouse contrasting with her short fair hair. 'I'm sorry to barge in. I didn't realise you had company,' she said, as Sasha struggled to overcome the power of Rex's devastating effect upon her. 'I only wanted to know if there was anything else you wanted taken back to the office . . .'

'Yes, Dee. There is.' He was the employer now, all competence and authority. 'But first . . . come in and meet the contemporary man's answer to Michelangelo.'

Both women laughed, Sasha somewhat shakily. Dee, she decided instantly, was nice.

'Sasha's finally helped me to decide how to take the starkness away from the recess,' Rex explained, giving her unnecessary credit. 'Sasha—meet my secretary, Dee Day.'

Putting down her brush, Sasha shook hands with the other woman, trying to conceal her amusement over the unfortunate name.

'Go ahead and smile.' Dee's own was understanding. 'Everyone else does. But when I met Mr Day I was more concerned with making my own conquest than with anyone else's!' Sasha had to laugh at that. Even Rex was enjoying the joke. 'Twenty-four years on and two lively adult teenagers later, I'm wondering whose victory it was—his or mine!'

Sasha laughed again, conscious of Rex's deep laughter beside her.

'Dee's reliable, efficient—and thoroughly prone to exaggeration,' came his amiable banter in response. 'But she also knows how to manipulate that husband and those children of hers—and her employer, too, sometimes.'

No, I don't think so, Sasha thought. If anyone did the manipulating it would be you. And a small prickle of awareness shivered down her spine so that before she knew it she was responding rather stiffly, 'Really? I wouldn't have thought anyone could do that.'

'Wise girl!' Dee approved smilingly. 'I can see you're obviously well-guarded against that fatal charm!'

'Yes,' Sasha breathed defiantly, and felt those disturbing grey eyes upon her, felt their sudden hostility even before he spoke.

'Take a break, Dee, while I get those things up together—and take Sasha with you. I know I've got a reputation for cracking a whip, but try to convince her that if she does her job well enough I'll probably not use it on her!'

Well, of all the...! Stunned by the change in his mood, Sasha turned, curbing a swift retort when she saw him already propelling himself away.

'Don't mind him—he's as curt with everyone,' remarked Dee in understanding tones, gesturing for Sasha to precede her into the garden. 'Ever since he had his accident anyway.'

Sasha caught her breath, unable to tell Dee that there was definitely more to his sudden flaying antagonism than that. 'How long have you worked for him?' she asked instead.

Dee guided her across the flags into the shrubbery, to a little stone seat set in a secluded nook. 'Ooh...' She pursed her lips, doing some mental arithmetic. 'It must be seven years now. I took the job as his PA just after his father died and Rex took over the company. He works from home a lot now—for obvious reasons—and I come and go whenever he wants anything done here, but most of the time you can find me at the London office. He's a great boss to work for, and despite what he said he doesn't actually stand over you with a whip.' She laughed. 'He is a perfectionist, though, and doesn't suffer inefficiency and incompetence lightly, but he's extremely fair and thoroughly appreciative of hard work. He's a hell of a guy,' she remarked softly, in a way that told Sasha that Rex's secretary was genuinely fond of her boss, 'but nowadays the only person he seems to be able to relax with is the lovely Lorraine Faraday, and even *she* seems to be trying his patience more these days.' Then, as an afterthought, 'Have you met Lorraine?'

Sasha's attention was fixed on an ornamental fountain, a light, silvery ribbon cascading down over the green-mossed stonework of a siren—a flawless creature, ageless, elegant.

'Yes. She's his cousin, isn't she?' she answered, feeling an inexplicable little cloud settling over her.

Dee's little chuckle sounded cynical. 'Of sorts. She's Rex's father's cousin's child—if you can work that one out—which I suppose makes her his second cousin. She's down here nearly every weekend. Twenty-two, very spoilt, very determined—*and* very successful. She's got her own beauty salon in Cambridge which Daddy set her up in and which she runs with the efficiency of someone twice her age, but what she really wants—and the thing she needs—is to marry Rex. Then she wouldn't get quite so much of her own way. At least then he might accept all the pampering she wants to give him—although I don't know if he'll ever fully accept what's happened to him. It has to be tough—confined to a wheelchair at only thirty-two. They said his last operation would give him a fifty-fifty chance of walking again—but I don't know…' Dee studied her feet in the high-heeled court shoes—stabbed a toe absently at the stone path. 'We're all beginning to lose hope and I think he is, too, although he hasn't actually admitted defeat. He only just suffers the physiotherapist, though, and he won't let anyone else help him with anything—except for Clem. So for Lorraine to change all that she'll have to be a miracle worker, although she's a very strong-willed girl and Rex does seem to enjoy her company. Anyway, you'll probably see her again tomorrow.' Dee pulled a wry face. 'As I said, she's down here most weekends.'

So why was she viewing the prospect with less than a little enthusiasm? Sasha asked of herself silently. She'd only seen Lorraine Faraday when she had come to after falling out of that basket, but even then she hadn't been particularly impressed.

'How nice,' she said to Dee, while berating herself for her decided lack of sincerity, although she had fewer recriminations when, true to Dee's prophesy, the other girl turned up, looking extravagantly casual, the following evening.

'Good heavens! Are you still here?' Lorraine exclaimed as she turned from hugging her aunt and saw Sasha coming from the garden room, across the magnificent hall.

'That's no way to greet your cousin's guest, darling,' Sheila remonstrated, far more indulgently, Sasha felt, than Lorraine deserved, as Rex's mother went on to explain why Sasha was there.

'Really?' A slim, bangled hand lifted to the chic fair hair with a strong waft of perfume, while the other hand held a pet basket containing, from what Sasha could gather from the sounds emanating loudly through the wicker, a very indignant cat. 'Rex didn't tell me.' She sounded as put out as the bundle of grey fur Sasha could see now through the grid of the basket, her gaze a penetrating, icy blue.

Surely Lorraine didn't see her as a rival? she thought then—and much later, after dinner, when they had adjourned to the luxury of the drawing-room and at Rex's insistence Sasha had tagged along as well.

'I haven't seen Rex for days. You'd think he'd want us to have *some* privacy, wouldn't you?' Lorraine, lounging on the sofa, laughed humourlessly at her aunt, leaving Sasha with the distinct impression that that remark was a direct dig at her.

'A total impossibility, little cousin,' Rex responded drily from across the room, 'when every time I have the pleasure of your company I also have to play host to that infernal cat.'

'Oh! Pharaoh isn't infernal, are you, sweety?' With a jingle of bangles, Lorraine pulled her pet down from where it had been sitting regally on the back of the settee, cradling it like a baby. 'You're callous, Rex,' she pouted sultrily, while the cat, part-Siamese, part-Russian blue, let out one of its typically Siamese yowls.

'Am I?' Amusement curved the firm male mouth, laughter lighting the grey eyes that clashed with Sasha's. Unexpectedly, something interrupted her heart's steady rhythm, and she responded with a small, conspiratorial smile. She loved animals, but this one was a real pain. And Rex had already witnessed the battle she had been having with it earlier, trying to keep it out of her tubs of paint.

Lorraine, however, had seen that collusive exchange, which was probably what prompted her suddenly to say, 'By the way, I saw the fresco you've started. It's quite good—if you like drawings all over your wall. Personally I would have kept the statue that belonged there instead of relegating it to the library. You don't appreciate classic beauty, Rex, that's your trouble.'

For a moment that masculine gaze strayed to Sasha, barely discernible, yet enough to evoke warm colour where it touched on the naturalness of her features, the pale skin above her gypsy-style blouse, before he drawled casually, glancing away, 'I wouldn't say that, Lorraine.'

Sasha's pulse throbbed. There had been unveiled sensuality in that cursory appraisal of her. But why, she thought, breathless, when her simple top and skirt made her feel like a bohemian beside Lorraine's salon chicness? And she noticed, from beneath the dark sable of her lashes, how tight-lipped the other girl looked.

'I still don't know why you moved it,' she was persisting rather sulkily, and then with another snipe at Sasha, 'A mural's all right if it's done well enough and in keeping, but quite frankly I don't think it has the sophistication of that statue.'

'Then take the bloody thing!' Rex's explosive retort shattered the air like a cannon, sending the cat careering from Lorraine's arms as he swung his chair powerfully away—out of the room.

'Oh, my dear, I'm sorry about that.' It was a tentative apology by Sheila in the tense little silence that followed.

'That's all right.' Sasha smiled to try and ease the woman's embarrassment, realising she had been holding her breath. So Rex had a temper—and how! she thought, darting a furtive glance across at Lorraine. She looked pale and upset, her lovely face taut with pique. As well it might be—taunting Rex like that! Sasha found herself siding with him, although she couldn't see why he should have exploded to such a degree over a simple statue. 'If you'll excuse me . . .'

Eager to get away from the animosity she could feel emanating from Lorraine Faraday, she had scarcely reached the door when she heard the girl say behind her—softly enough so that her aunt wouldn't hear, 'He won't appreciate it, you know—running after him when he's in one of these moods. But if you're so keen to get your head bitten off—go ahead.'

Unable to believe what she was hearing, stiffly Sasha returned over her shoulder, 'I'm not running after him, Lorraine.' Good heavens! She hardly knew the man. 'I just prefer to stay out of domestic squabbles—particularly between cousins,' she was unable to stop herself adding rather pointedly, a remark that prompted Lorraine to retaliate swiftly with,

'It was hardly a domestic squabble. I thought we were having a cultural discussion. And anyway, he's not my real cousin,' she stressed, reiterating what Sasha had learned from Dee only the previous day. And Lorraine just had to make that point, Sasha realised, knowing instinctively that the other girl was saying, He's mine—keep off! before Lorraine brushed past her with a rather cloying stab of perfume.

Intending to go upstairs, but seeing Lorraine going in the same direction, not wanting to involve herself in any further clashes with the young beautician, Sasha held back, lingering in the stately grandeur of the hall.

She wasn't sure where Rex had gone, presuming it would have been to his own suite. The door to the library was open, however, and something drew her inside. The statue, she decided, if she were honest with herself, and which had been the subject of such bitter conflict between Rex and Lorraine.

It stood there, on a low chest, just inside the door, a subtle glow from a pair of red wall-shades throwing a rosy hue over the white marble.

'Terpsichore'. Sasha read the name engraved on the base of the marble. Wasn't she the daughter of Zeus? One of the nine muses, she remembered from her Greek mythology, her puzzling brain working it out. Of course, the goddess of dancing! And then everything became clear.

How insensitive of Lorraine not to have realised, she thought—not to have understood why Rex must have wanted it removed. The lithe beauty of the figure, every delicately sculpted limb, portrayed grace and movement—the mobility of which he had been denied.

'Did your inquisitiveness get the better of you, Sasha?'

She spun round so fast that she almost collided with the open door. He'd been in the room all the time, just behind it, and she hadn't realised!

'I—I was just curious,' she stammered, taking in the other features of the room, the book-lined walls and the polished table in the centre, the huge fireplace, and the rich brocade of the sofa and easy-chairs.

'Naturally.' His tone was clipped. 'Well, since you're here, come in.' It was the most ungallant invitation she had ever had in her life and she started as he picked up a cane that had been resting against one of the bookcases and pushed forcefully at the door, slamming it shut. 'Come in and entertain me,' he said abrasively, and when she still didn't move, 'Oh, come on, Sasha. I would have thought you were mature enough not to sulk like my rather too pampered little cousin. Perhaps too mature—too serious, in some ways.'

She frowned, uneasy, feeling as if he could see through to her innermost thoughts and feelings.

'I'm not going to eat you,' he conveyed with sudden gentle mockery, a weary smile appeasing the dark turbulence of his features.

'I'd hardly have thought you were,' Sasha responded more courageously, moving away from the chest, 'since we *have* only just had dinner.'

Her witticism evoked a warmer smile from him. 'Hardly a guarantee,' he drawled, turning his chair as she wandered interestedly towards one of the huge bookcases. 'Even I've been known to indulge in seconds if the dessert's irresistible enough.'

She looked at him cagily, her pulses racing. He had positioned himself between the fireplace and the sofa, elbows resting on that cane laid across his chair. His eyes were darkly reflective as they met the wary blue of hers, and a line deepened between his as he asked suddenly, 'Are you afraid of me?'

Sasha caught her breath, her blood rushing through her. 'Should I be?' she uttered, lifting her chin in unconscious rebellion.

'You're darn right you should!'

The cane he tossed down with more than vehement force made her jump, and he laughed, a hard, mirthless sound from deep in his chest. 'So now you know I have vulnerabilities.' That harsh male pride was making her pay for discovering his weakness over that sculpture. 'Be a good girl and don't pass it on to Lorraine. My cousin believes I'm a tower of invincible strength. I'd hate to disillusion her. But don't underestimate me, Sasha, or show a gram of pity, or I'll crush you with me. As it stands, sometimes I think you're the only source of stimulation to me in this whole darn house!'

The slow tick of a grandfather clock made mockery of the way her heart was suddenly thudding. But why? Just because an attractive man had just paid her a compliment—albeit in the most uncomplimentary way! she thought, almost jumping with fright as Pharaoh—mewing loudly—seemed to spring from nowhere on to Rex's shoulder.

'There's another!' Her laughter trembled, but only through shock, she convinced herself, wondering how Rex had managed to stay so calm, so cool as he tried to extricate the clinging animal from around his neck.

'Have you ever tried barbecued cat?' His dry cynicism suggested that he would dearly love to—if only with Pharaoh, although those strong hands were gentle with the furry creature, and now laughter-lines at the corners of his eyes were alleviating the strain in the handsome face as he suggested, 'Or perhaps he'd prefer being mummified!'

'I don't think Lorraine would appreciate hearing you say that,' Sasha laughed back, secretly thanking Pharaoh for easing the tension between them as the cat scrambled out of his arms, leapt on to a table and disappeared behind the settee. 'Oh, well...' She shrugged, moving back to the door.

'Wait a minute.'

The deep-voiced command stopped her in her tracks. 'I came in to get a book, but I see someone's put it rather out of my reach. That thick volume...' He gestured towards the bookcase across the room, opposite the fireplace. 'On that third shelf above the cupboard. Would you be a good girl and get it down for me?'

Why was it that even that soft modulation of his voice should make her sinews quiver? she thought, cautioning herself as she complied readily, remembering what Dee had said about his refusing help from anyone. Was he making concessions in her case? she considered, questioning a ridiculous surge of inner warmth as she lifted the heavy book down from the shelf.

'Have you read it?'

He'd noticed her cursory interest in the title—a book by a best-selling author—but she shook her head. 'I read one of his when I was at college. It was OK, but nothing I could get too excited about,' she confessed, crossing the room.

'Oh? And what exactly does it take to excite you, Sasha?'

He meant literature, of course. So why were her cheeks burning—her hands shaking as she handed him the book? she wondered, hoping he wouldn't notice—and she might have got away with it if Pharaoh hadn't darted under her feet just as she was stepping back, so that with a little cry of alarm she stumbled against the settee, grasping at anything to save herself before ending up on the soft brocade of the arm.

Mortified, she realised then that it was Rex's sleeve she had grasped, and that it was only those quick reflexes of that strong arm still around her that had somehow broken her fall.

'Are you all right?'

'Yes.' It was a breathless, trembling response.

'Then why are you shaking?'

'I'm not. I...' She looked up at him and that dark and vibrant sexuality seemed to liquefy her bones. 'It was the cat.'

'Liar,' he breathed, and she knew a sudden gushing in her ears as the next moment he dragged her to him, his face going out of focus as his mouth came demandingly down on hers.

It seemed an eternity since a man had kissed her and, caught off guard, she could do nothing but submit, rocked by the hard, intimate contact of his body, by the unbelievable strength in his arms. She uttered some small sound as his tongue slid between her lips, the hard persuasion calling to some part of her she had thought had died, igniting a spark of dormant desire way, way down inside. She could feel its warmth coursing along her veins, the familiar tension of physical need building in her loins. The arm of his chair was pressing into her, hurting her, but she didn't care, her arms going around him, her lips parting willingly for him now so that, without conscious volition, desperately she was kissing him back. Her heart was light, her senses wild and soaring, striving to rise above the clouds of guilt-ridden grief, of treacherous, torturous betrayal...

'No!' It took all of her strength to push away from him, her eyes dark with turmoil, with desire. 'No, I can't!'

The taut lines of Rex's face conveyed desire as real as her own, desire and an almost hurt bewilderment, and now she saw an ugly emotion cut across his mouth, cold as the sculpted marble of the muse.

'I'm sorry,' he breathed in a hard, ragged tone. 'I hadn't realised how repulsive it must be for you—being kissed by a cripple.'

Oh, God! Was that what he thought?

Her hand went to her lips in horror. 'It isn't . . . I mean I . . .'

Breathing as irregularly as he was, she saw the chilling emotion in his eyes, hopelessness, guilt and remorse tearing her away from him, up to the merciful isolation of her own room.

Oh, heaven! How could she have let him kiss her like that—respond to him as she had when she was still in love with Ben? she wondered through an agony of remorse, leaning back against the door, closing her eyes. And when she'd promised herself she would never get involved with anyone again. Was she so easy? Had Ben meant so little to her—and after she'd been responsible for his death—that she could feel such a strong physical attraction to Rex Templeton?

Not wanting even to think about it, she forced herself to take a shower, willing the soothing warmth of the water to erase the memory of his arms around her, of her devastating response to his kiss. What it couldn't erase, however, was the knowledge that was tearing through her, that, far from the revulsion he had accused her of experiencing, for a few frightening moments with him she had felt a desire stronger than anything she had ever felt before in her life.

Rex wasn't around when she came down to breakfast the following morning, neither was Lorraine, and Sasha could only assume that the two of them must have gone out together.

Why, then, had he kissed her like that when he had such an obviously willing companion in the younger girl? she wondered with an emotion she refused to give a name to. Had she herself been merely a diversion since he had quarrelled with his lovely cousin?

Just a means of boosting that arrogant male ego—
which must understandably have been weakened by
his accident—to see if he could make her respond to
him, and which he might have realised had been
shockingly true if he hadn't so wrongly interpreted
her ultimate rejection of him last night?

Well, let them enjoy themselves together! she
thought, feeling stupidly hurt, and, trying to put the
memory of that kiss out of her mind, she offered some
lame explanation to Sheila for eating very little
breakfast and, making her excuses, went back
upstairs.

She was still deciding whether to stay in and get on
with her fresco, or drive into town, when a cat's
plaintive crying coming from what she could only
deduce was—unbelievably!—outside her window
stopped her in her tracks.

Crossing the room, Sasha flung open the casement
and looked out. The cat was crouched a little way
along the deep ornamental ledge that ran beneath her
window, its wide amber eyes and pathetic wails evi-
dence that it was afraid.

'You've really tackled something beyond your
capabilities this time, haven't you, puss?' she laughed.
But how on earth had it got there? So far above the
ground? Not from inside, she thought, because, noticing the window-cleaner's ladder out there earlier,
she'd closed the window before she'd gone downstairs
to make things easier for him. Unless . . .

'You climbed the *ladder*?' she exhaled, only believing it through remembering another cat which used
to do the same thing. 'You climbed the ladder—but
you couldn't get back down!'

A mournful wail was all her clever process of deduction was rewarded with, and after a few gentle words of encouragement to try and coax the cat inside it became obvious that Pharaoh was far too frightened to move. And that left her with only one alternative— to get out there and bring him in herself!

It'll be all right—if I don't look down, she thought, and kept on reminding herself as she eased herself gingerly out of the window and, on hands and knees, began edging her way along the ledge. Really, it was wide enough to walk on, she assured herself. It was only the thought of being up so high.

It wasn't doing the knees of her jeans much good either, she realised wryly, closing her eyes, breath held, as a piece of the crumbling ledge gave way and fell, splintering with an ominous clatter on to the terrace way below. Eventually, though, she managed to reach the terrified animal, making a grab for it with one hand and, clutching its solid little body to her, started edging backwards towards the safety of her window.

The throb of an engine reached her ears and she chanced a glimpse below. A metallic-blue sports car was coming up the drive. Rex—with Lorraine Faraday at the wheel!

She heard the car pull up, the sound of voices, a door close and after some time another, but she didn't look down; not until she had reached her window and could stand up straight. And then she wished she hadn't when she saw Lorraine and Clem looking disbelievingly up at her, and Rex, on his crutches now, staring up at her with a look that could have slain.

'What the hell do you think you're doing?' His anger was almost as daunting as her climb along the ledge, a hard, palpable force that split the air above the terrace as he commanded, *'Get back inside*!'

She didn't need his incensed order to make her glad to feel carpet beneath her feet again as, dropping Pharaoh through the window first, she swung her legs over the sill into her room.

'If I didn't know you were a dumb animal, I'd think you'd enticed me out there deliberately to make him mad at me,' she told the cat, who had immediately skulked off under her bed, and only then realised that she was shaking. She hadn't been that frightened, had she? she thought, with a measure of surprise. Or was it merely a reaction to Rex's anger that had made her legs feel so wobbly?

Well, at least he can't come up here and lambaste me for it, she found a guilty relief in realising, since the lift he'd finally succumbed to admitting he needed to make his life easier hadn't yet been finished. Nor could it have been better timed, she thought, when Sheila buzzed through to tell her that Gavin Chase was on the line. Gavin was back in Suffolk for the weekend and wanted to know if he could pick her up in half an hour.

'Great! That will be lovely,' she told him, glad that he didn't comment on how breathless she sounded. She didn't feel like explaining. And she certainly didn't want to admit to being so strongly affected by Rex.

Ringing off, and noticing the chalky patches on the knees of her jeans, hastily she changed into some pale lemon dungarees and a matching short-sleeved shirt and then, not wishing to see anyone, went hurriedly downstairs to wait for Gavin outside.

She had almost reached the front door without meeting a soul, but a door off the hall was ajar and as she passed Rex's voice came through the aperture, hard and inexorable.

'Sasha! Come in here.'

She stopped dead, her pulse-rate increasing, her mouth suddenly feeling dry. Did he know her step so well that he could distinguish it from that of his mother? Lorraine? Or any female member of his staff?

She found the thought strangely unnerving, taking a deep breath before going in.

It was his office, which she hadn't seen until now. Sitting at his desk, he didn't even look up immediately, engrossed in some papers which he was slipping into a drawer. Another desk held a word processor— where Dee worked, Sasha guessed—while beyond that filing cabinets and paper-stacked shelves designated this room as a hive of commercial enterprise, although all she was aware of at that moment was the sound of that drawer closing, and the intensity of suppressed emotion in Rex's face as he finally looked up.

'What the devil did you think you were doing— climbing about up there on that ledge?'

He spoke with a quiet anger, all the more daunting now because it was so controlled, and as she started to answer, 'Rescuing Lorraine's——' one of his hands came down so hard on the desk that she staggered back in fear.

'So you're not totally lacking in the instinct of self-preservation,' he derided coldly, noting that nervous reaction, 'though quite honestly you could have fooled me. However, if you *are* so hell-bent on trying to kill yourself, could you do me the courtesy of not being so damned determined to accomplish it on my property?'

'I wasn't trying to kill myself!' Colour stained her throat and cheeks as she snapped out her angry defence. 'Pharaoh climbed up the ladder——'

'And like a good little Samaritan you just had to get out there and rescue it.'

'Yes!'

'You little fool! Don't you realise how old this place is? How dangerous those ledges are? Go out and take a look at the pieces of stone all over the terrace if you don't believe me.'

Sasha shuddered, refusing to think about what could have happened. Anyway, it didn't give Rex the right to be speaking to her as he was!

'I'm sorry. I'll sweep them up if you'll give me——'

'Don't try and evade the issue.'

'Well, I couldn't leave him there!' she protested, when he was giving her no quarter. 'He was terrified!'

'Then you should have asked Clem or some other male member of the staff to help you. Not go crawling around on ledges on your hands and knees like the heroine of some . . . some Gothic novel!'

'By which time the cat might have panicked and injured itself—or something worse,' she argued, opposing his implacable will with a taut-faced determination of her own.

'It wouldn't have been that stupid.'

And she had been—that was what he meant.

Across the desk, her gaze met and locked with his, and she caught her breath, feeling the unwelcome tug of that frightening chemistry that had brought about that slow, sensual reawakening in her, that guilt-ridden response to him the previous night. And if she were honest with herself she would have to admit that that was why she had so readily accepted Gavin's invitation—to put a barrier between her and her unwilling attraction to Rex Templeton.

Even so, that attraction wouldn't be denied, and she felt a deep ache in the pit of her stomach when his gaze dropped to her lips and he said softly, 'What sort of girl risks life and limb to save a cat she doesn't even know?'

Sasha's head lifted slightly, an insurgent little gesture in response to the feeling she was trying desperately to deny. 'I thought you'd already assessed that. A stupid one,' she uttered poignantly.

His jaw seemed to clench from some inner conflict, and his nostrils dilated, etching those arrogant features with harsh lines. 'Hardly that,' he drawled with a chafing cynicism, and it took Sasha a few moments to realise why. Was it because of last night? Because he'd thought she'd objected to his kisses because he was crippled?

Part of her ached to deny it, tell him that that wasn't true at all. But he hadn't actually mentioned the previous night and she didn't have the confidence to raise the subject herself, and so all she said in a well-controlled voice was, 'No,' despairing when she realised how cold it sounded, saw from the harsh emotion on his face that she had only strengthened his belief.

Hopelessly, she watched him tap the gold pen impatiently on the desk.

'What are you intending to do today?' His face was a granite mask now, all emotion erased. And when she hesitated, reluctant to condemn herself further in his eyes by telling him she was going out with Gavin, he said, 'Lorraine's going riding this afternoon. Do you want to join her? Needless to say I shan't be taking part in that little exercise, but we've arranged to meet for a meal in the village afterwards if you're interested.'

Sasha hesitated, wondering if the invitation had come solely from him, because she couldn't imagine Lorraine having anything to do with it. She'd been intending to go riding, too—ever since Sheila had told her to make use of the stables—but not with Lorraine Faraday for company. And so, essaying a polite smile, she said only, 'Thank you. But I've already made plans for today.'

As if to reinforce her statement, Gavin's company car could be heard coming up the drive, and Rex's lips thinned as the vehicle pulled up outside the window.

'So I see,' he snarled as the other man got out. 'You've obviously far less sense than I credited you with. I would have thought you better principled than to invite the attentions of a social-climbing materialist like Chase.'

His tone was scathing as he brought his chair around the desk, prompting Sasha's heated, 'I'm not inviting his attentions!'

'No?' Mockery gave a cruel curve to that sensual mouth. 'And are you saying you didn't invite mine?'

That raw, insidious awareness stole menacingly through her blood. He was too close, his dangerous proximity firing a series of warning signals to her brain.

'That was different. It was an accident. I—I tripped . . .'

'And fell right into my arms!' His teeth showed white as he laughed harshly, making her nerve-ends quiver. 'I'd be careful, Sasha. Some accidents have a way of producing repercussions that we might not necessarily welcome.'

Intimating what? she wondered, feeling that naked sexual tension stretching between them as his gaze slid over her, so that with her cheeks flaming she said pointedly, 'Will that be all?'

He didn't deign to give her an answer, just one slaying look from him sending her flying from his office as though her feet were wings.

'So how's it going?' Gavin enquired when they were motoring away from the Halt, and, grateful for his company, Sasha began to relax.

She'd been right to agree to see him, she thought. He was the diversion she needed to take her mind off Rex and he didn't intrude on her personal feelings in the way the other man did.

'That's great,' he said when she finished bringing him up to date with her fresco, although he didn't sound as enamoured with her progress as his initial interest had implied, and she realised why when he said, 'It is. But what I really meant was what's it like living with the Templetons?' Smilingly, he winked at her across the car's interior. 'Have you got me an invitation to dinner yet?'

He was joking, of course, but, disappointed, she had to force herself to laugh in response. 'Is that the only reason you wanted me to keep in touch?'

'Naturally.' He laughed out loud, glancing across at her, then back at the road again. 'Don't be silly. I happen to fancy you like mad, Sasha *Margan*.'

She shrank from his rather brash imitation of her accent, uneasy, too, that he might be getting too serious about her. And it must have showed in her face because suddenly he said, 'I'm not looking for involvement, if that's what you're afraid of. I'm just looking for the same things you are. Fun. Relaxation. To get what I can out of life—for the time being anyway.'

Except that she wasn't looking for anything, she thought. She was still trying to repair the shattered fragments of her life. But more lightly than she felt she murmured, 'And a more formal introduction to Rex Templeton!'

'Most definitely!' Gavin grinned, fortunately too busy overtaking a learner driver to notice the sudden tension in her. 'And perhaps an introduction to that gorgeous blonde I saw coming across the terrace.' Back on the right side of the road, he sent a mischievous glance her way. 'Only joking, of course. Seriously, though, who was she?' he asked, more interested, Sasha guessed, then he was letting on.

When she told him, he whistled under his breath and said, 'So that's Lorraine Faraday! What a cracker! And you say she visits every weekend? Very magnanimous of a cousin—second, third or however many times removed she might happen to be. With a come-on like that—plus those looks—old Templeton's gotta be interested. She spells money, too—and there's really nothing quite like keeping it in the family, is there?'

His deductions only coincided, if a little more crudely, with Dee's. So why did Gavin's make her feel so piqued?

'How can you say that just by looking at someone?' She felt argumentative, too. 'For all you know he might not be the slightest bit interested in her in that way,' she suggested heatedly, feeling a surprisingly strong compulsion to convince him.

'Oh, I see.' His eyes shifted from the road, narrowing, perceptive. 'Is that what you're hoping?' he asked.

'Don't be silly.' Of course it wasn't, and if her pulse was thumping it was only with annoyance through Gavin's suggesting it.

'He's rich,' he said, almost persuasively.

'Means nothing.' This with a dismissive gesture of her hands.

'And handsome.'

Again that dismissal. 'Only skin-deep.'

'And he's got a sex appeal that no woman I know of who's come into contact with him has ever been able to resist.' Jealousy coloured his voice. In spite of what he'd been saying earlier, Gavin minded!

'Well, *I* can!' Why did it need so much vehemence on her part to convince him? Was it because she was so aware herself of that ruthlessly potent attraction? That smouldering sexuality that had almost ensnared her last night?

She took a deep breath and changed the subject. She had no particular interest in Rex Templeton, so what were they doing arguing about him anyway? She had come out to try and enjoy herself—or at least to take her mind off things, she thought wistfully, although later, after Gavin had brought her back to the Halt and driven off, she felt ungrateful to discover that she hadn't really enjoyed herself at all— and it was useless pretending she didn't know the reason why.

Rex was affecting her more profoundly than she wanted to admit and that scene with him in his office earlier had thoroughly depressed her. His cynicism had cut into her like barbed wire, and she knew it was because of the previous night, yet not in a million years could she begin to explain to him. To do that she would have to bare her soul—tell him everything. And her memories were too torturous—her guilt too strong to share with anyone; least of all, she realised hopelessly, with a man like him.

CHAPTER FOUR

DAY by day the fresco was taking on more and more life, the golden grasses and ripe corn seeming to sway in an unseen breeze, the soft hues complementing the red splashes of watercolour flowers now taking recognisable shape through Sasha's loving skill.

She had never been commissioned to paint anything so extensive before and she was pleased with her efforts, putting as much time into it as she could.

'Anyone would think I kept a ball and chain around your ankle. You're supposed to be on holiday,' Rex reminded her drily one afternoon during the following week, looking in before his physiotherapist was due to arrive. 'Correct me if I'm wrong—but I'm sure I heard you in here just after six.'

He was looking at the fresco with a studied absorption, watching the feather-fine strokes of her brush creating a little red miracle in the perfect facsimile of a poppy. As he had promised, though, he didn't say anything, and with butterflies in her stomach Sasha wondered what he was thinking.

'I just want to get it finished,' she said a little jerkily, as keen as he was to see the end result. 'After that I'll start relaxing.'

'And you'll have earned your keep and therefore won't feel so indebted to me.'

Sasha looked at him quickly, the red-tipped brush suspended in mid-air. 'I didn't mean that,' she said, colouring. 'I meant——'

66

'No?' An eyebrow arched in mocking scepticism. Of course, he was far too clever to be fooled.

'Well, you must admit it's only natural,' she justified, resuming her work with gusto because he was making a study now of her figure beneath her scoop-necked T-shirt and shorts, and because ever since that night in the library he had only to enter a room to make her shatteringly conscious of him. A purely chemical reaction of female to sexually attractive male, she reasoned logically, which that kiss had somehow dangerously exaggerated.

'Don't let me stop you,' he surprised her by saying rather curtly then, and wheeled himself abruptly away to prepare for his therapy.

Deciding it would be a good time to take a break, Sasha went off to get some coffee, taking it into the garden to drink, alone on the little stone seat, as it was such a lovely day.

When she returned to the garden room, the physiotherapist had already arrived. She could hear the woman's patient, muffled tones through the wall; movement, and the occasional deep curse from Rex.

Later, there came the sound of water running in the adjoining bathroom, then, some time after, the closing of a door in the hall as the physiotherapist left.

After that, Sasha's ears were unconsciously tuned to every small sound from next door—the customary squeak of the wheelchair, the clack of crutches being laid down and the sudden creak of the bed yielding beneath that demanding weight. Another indistinguishable sound was followed by a muttered invective, and, trying to keep her mind on the ochre leaf she was painting, Sasha felt a deep ache of compassion.

How did such a strong man cope with being so severely impeded? she wondered. Especially an independent, hard-headed character like Rex.

The internal telephone ringing on its little cane table made her jump, and her heart skipped a beat when, picking it up, she heard Rex's deep voice at the other end.

'Sasha—can you help me, please?'

He sounded composed enough. Nevertheless, quickly Sasha dropped her brush and hurried into the adjoining room.

In light boxer shorts—all he was wearing on his lower torso—and a fine white shirt, gaping to the waist, he was sitting on the bed and he looked up, frowning, as she came in.

'I'm sorry.' He sounded offhand, clearly aware of the shock she knew had manifested itself on her face. 'I really didn't realise it would offend you.'

'It doesn't,' Sasha said quickly, tearing her gaze from the sinewy olive of his chest and those hair-shadowed, heavily-muscled legs. Of course it didn't matter. So why did her tongue seem to be sticking to the roof of her mouth?

'I dropped a cuff-link——' his chin jerked forward slightly '—under the bed. I tried to get it myself but I'm afraid it's too far out of reach.'

'That's no problem.' She had to get down on her hands and knees, and then grope around under the low-sprung divan, feeling over the carpet until she found it. 'How did it get this far. . . ?' Too far under simply to have rolled there, she thought, puzzled. And then noticed the cane discarded beside those tanned feet and guessed that the link must have fallen in the other direction and in exasperation he'd probably used too much angry force in trying to retrieve it. 'Were you getting impatient with it?' Her smile was a gentle reproof as she got to her feet.

'Good gracious, woman!' It was a harmlessly chiding growl. 'You're beginning to sound like my nurse!'

'Heaven forbid!' Sasha laughed, handing him the cuff-link, wanting to lighten his mood, ease his irritability. 'With a patient like you, I wouldn't enjoy that job at all!'

'Pity,' he drawled, with a glint appearing in those heavily fringed eyes, and now that brooding mouth took on the barest of smiles. 'From this side of the fence I think I could rather enjoy it.'

Sasha blushed, trying not to think about the sort of things being his nurse would entail, watching him securing the cuff-link—the only man she knew who wore them—black onyx set in gold, striking against the stark whiteness of his cuff. 'Frescos are demanding enough,' she laughed, more nervously this time, and, turning away, heard his voice, deep and low behind her.

'Don't go.'

She looked at him enquiringly, her adrenalin racing.

'Come and sit down.' He patted the bed beside him. 'Here.'

With her breath locking in her lungs, stiffly Sasha complied.

'You're working too hard,' he remonstrated softly, and unexpectedly caught her chin between his thumb and forefinger, studying her with electrifying intensity. 'You look pale. Is anything troubling you?'

The scent of his cologne clung to his hand, his touch sending sensations through her that produced an instinctive withdrawal, one she was only aware of when he breathed hoarsely, 'Do I repulse you that much?'

Bitterness twisted his mouth, making Sasha swallow. Whatever the consequences, she had to tell him.

'No,' she murmured, keeping her gaze lowered. 'You don't repulse me at all.'

He laughed then, quite harshly, at her tremulous admission. 'You say that? Sitting on a man's bed? You really do believe in courting danger, don't you?'

Derisively he turned away, reaching for his watch on the bedside chest.

'No, I just believe in telling the truth,' Sasha said steadily, watching him fasten the dark strap around that very masculine wrist.

'No matter where it may lead?' His gaze flitted sceptically over her. 'Or perhaps you think you're safe—sitting here with somehow less of a man than the Gavin Chases of this world; is that it?'

Sasha took a deep breath. 'I didn't say that—you did.'

'Yes,' he exhaled through gritted teeth, fixing his other cuff.

His pain was a palpable thing, and, not a stranger to anguish herself, Sasha silently sympathised, her gaze unconsciously straying to his legs. There was a long, jagged scar on one of those sinewy thighs—in addition, of course, to the injuries he'd obviously sustained to his back—interrupting the smooth covering of hair, and on impulse she wanted to reach out and touch that perfect, powerless limb, caress the white, marring line of that scar, only just managing to stop herself in time.

'Are ... things getting any better?' she queried tentatively instead. Hadn't Dee said he'd had a fifty-fifty chance of walking again?

'Let's just say I shan't be climbing any mountains,' he said cynically.

'I'm sorry.' Without thinking she touched his arm and felt the muscle flex, the tension that brought his breath dragging through his lungs, and she gave a small gasp, unprepared for the response her unconscious action produced as, with a sudden twist of his body, he pushed her down on to the bed.

'Are you?' His voice was hard, lips mocking her shocked response though his face was slashed with lines of bitter turmoil. 'Well, pity isn't what I need, Sasha—I'm a man, for goodness' sake! And you're very aware of that fact, aren't you?' he breathed, his gaze probing the wary depths of hers. 'More aware, I think, than you're actually prepared to admit—no matter what you might say to the contrary.'

'No.' It was a small, gasped utterance, more in protest at the lips that had found the throbbing hollow at her throat, the line that marked the gentle valley between her breasts.

His hair brushed against her skin, feather-light, deadly arousing.

No, please ... ! Gritting her teeth, she closed her eyes and sank her nails into the duvet to contain the responses that were shuddering through her. She couldn't! Not with him—not with any man! She didn't deserve to love—not after what she'd done to Ben!

Pain ravaged her face, a testimony to the havoc of desire and guilt that was raging in her, and suddenly she became aware that those insidiously sweet kisses had stopped.

Opening her eyes, she saw Rex looking down at her, his face harshly drawn from the desire he'd been holding in check, though his eyes were glittering like ice.

'For God's sake! Get out of here,' he said in a savage whisper.

His mood was so menacing that she didn't wait to be told a second time, choking back a sob as she stumbled back into the garden room and out through the double doors.

If she'd wanted him to go on thinking that he repelled her then she couldn't have done a better job! she thought, hating herself. But how could she tell him that inside she was as crippled as he was—emotionally if not physically? She'd made him despise her—and it served her right! she acknowledged bitterly, feeling the tears biting behind her eyes.

Blindly, taking deep breaths to stem the raw pain burning inside her, she skirted the garden, subsequently finding herself beside the long, low outbuildings of the stables at the side of the house.

Large questing heads peered out over the stable doors, the evocative scent of horse and leather greeting her with the gentle stamping of hoofs—the occasional soft whinny, answered from another animal in a neighbouring stall.

'Do you want something to ride?' The surly Clem startled her, emerging from one of the stables, his weathered features crowned as usual by the familiar cap. 'There's the roan, or the chestnut.' He jerked a glance across the courtyard. 'Or that bay over there.'

All beautiful horses. But Sasha was drawn to a large dappled grey looking out of the end stall. Seventeen hands of powerful gelding whose great muscular flanks she could see surging with restless power as she approached.

'I wouldn't go near him—that's no woman's horse.' Clem's discriminating tones drifted across to her with the clip-clop of hoofs as he led a sleek, saddled chestnut out of another stable. 'That's Mr Rex's horse. It's only me that rides him now—consequently he doesn't get as much exercise as he should. It makes him edgy. Do you want me to saddle something for you, or can you manage?'

'I can manage,' Sasha answered distractedly, pleased that when she reached up to stroke the huge dappled nose the horse didn't pull away.

Why, though, if there was so little chance of Rex walking again, did he keep it? she wondered feelingly, and might have asked Clem if she hadn't found him so churlish, absently acknowledging him when he gave a sideways jerk of his head and said bluntly, 'In that case, tack-room's through there,' and without another word led the chestnut away.

'Steady, boy.' She patted the gelding's warm neck as it shifted restlessly again. Its ears were forward, picking up the sound of the chestnut's trotting hoofs, and it tossed its head, stamping a protest against the confines of its stall.

'Missing your master, boy?' Fearlessly, Sasha cupped its chin, laying her dark head sympathetically against the creature's muzzle. Did it ache inside as much as she did? Feel as desolate and confused without that controlling hand as she felt right now?

An emptiness, more crushing than any she had known before, overwhelmed her, and, feeling a strange affinity with the gelding, quickly she found its tack.

She was used to horses. Her best friend's uncle had owned a ranch in Texas and many school vacations had been spent racing Juliet across the dusty range.

This creature was different, though, from the gentle ponies she had known then—seventeen hands of pure muscle. *And* determination, she realised with a small, challenging thrill when they were clear of the vicinity of the house on the bridle-path that skirted the ad-joining golf course, and she was able to give it its head.

The dark ochre of cut rape and the lush green of a spinach crop stretched away on the other side, all once Templeton land, she had learned only the other day, but sold off gradually, piece by piece, over the years. The late afternoon sun was warm on her bare limbs, turning a striped, partially harvested field of ripe wheat to a carpet of bronze and gold. She could see the steady progress of a tractor at its work, smell the fragrance of freshly baled hay drifting up from the valley, its scent sweet and redolent on the air.

'Whoa, boy!' She wasn't sure how far she had come when she eventually drew rein, her earlier dejection eased by some good hard exercise and fresh air. The gelding had burnt off its surplus energies, too, she thought, until she turned its head for home, and sud-denly she found she was battling to keep the animal under control.

'Whoa, there!' Thrusting her feet hard forward in the stirrups, she wrestled with the reins, struggling to keep the horse from bolting away. It was too strong, too wilful and just too plain determined, though, to heed to her futile feminine demands, and Sasha gave a frightened cry as it suddenly reared up, tossing her backwards over a low wooden fence so that she made a soft but ungainly landing into the harvested wheat.

Winded, but unhurt, she struggled to her feet, just in time to see the horse, with its reins and stirrups flying, rounding the bend in the narrow country road and out of sight.

Brushing herself down, Sasha looked after it in dismay. It might find its own way back safely—but what if it didn't? What if it got into someone's field and started eating their crops? Or, worse, ran into the path of a car and caused an accident?

Her blood running cold, without wasting another second she was back over the fence and giving chase, stopping breathlessly after a while when she realised the futility of the exercise. The horse could be miles away by now. It could already be halfway back to the Halt, which meant that she'd have no chance of getting back herself before anyone realised what had happened. No, not just anyone—Rex, she thought, shuddering, deciding she had done enough as it was to alienate herself in his eyes without this as well.

Concern for the horse more than for herself, however, meant she had to get back as quickly as possible—and there was only one way to do that.

It was some time before she heard a vehicle coming, and, pausing to catch her breath, rather self-consciously held out her thumb. She'd never hitched a ride in her life! And obviously she didn't have the knack, she thought, despairing, as the car passed without stopping, and after a few seconds another, leaving her jogging hopelessly along the quiet road.

Third time lucky? she prayed, hearing another car coming, hardly believing her luck when, before she had even glanced round, she heard the car slowing down. Turning to smile, her expression changed to shocked recognition as she watched the back passenger door of the BMW swing open.

'Well, what a surprise.' There was something dangerously accommodating in Rex's voice, in his face, as she slid on to the seat beside him. What quirk of fate had decreed that it should be *him* who had to stop and pick her up? she thought with her heart sinking. She hadn't even realised he'd gone out. And if Clem had been saddling that chestnut for Sheila and hadn't been back to the stables, then he wouldn't yet have missed the gelding . . . 'Rex, I——'

'Been enjoying the delights of rural Suffolk?' That dangerously forced urbanity cut across her nervous attempt to explain, although the gaze tugging over her held a steely quality, contradicting his smile. 'What the hell do you think you're doing?' he rasped quietly over the deep purr of the engine.

Sasha's throat worked nervously. 'You mean hitchhiking?' Well, what else could he mean? she thought, wondering why that should make him sound so angry, wondering, too, how she was going to tell him. 'I wasn't sure where I was—how to get back. Rex, I know this——'

She broke off, tensing as his sleeve lightly grazed her bare arm and she felt him pulling something out of her hair.

'Either you've been making love in a hay-stack,' he said in a dangerously soft voice, twirling the piece of dry straw between his fingers, 'or that spirited animal of mine threw you. It would make an interesting deduction either way, wouldn't it, Clem?'

So he already knew! 'I——' She faltered, intimidated by the grim set of his profile, and from the driver's seat she heard Clem drawl laconically, incriminating her, 'I warned her it was dangerous—that he wasn't fit for a woman.'

'Did you now?' Those softly breathed words of Rex's promised recompense, despite the tight smile playing around his mouth.

'Rex, I'm sorry.' It was a vain attempt to dispel the raw anger she could feel emanating from him, but he wasn't even looking at her now. He was looking intently at the rear-view mirror, which Clem seemed to be giving more visual attention than was necessary.

'You won't mind if I get a paper?' he said, pulling into a lay-by in the pretty village they were just passing through, and Sasha tensed, hearing the hand-brake click into place, realising what had been going on. There had been a silent instruction by Rex through that mirror that had told Clem, I'll deal with this alone, and the older man had dutifully complied, she thought, swallowing as the driver's door was thrown closed and she was left to face Rex's anger alone.

'What the hell did you think you were playing at—taking a horse you knew you couldn't control—without even telling anyone where you were going? Did you think no one would notice when it came back alone—in a hell of a lather? Or were you crazy enough to think you could handle it all by yourself?'

'I said I'm sorry!' she threw back, trying to convince him, while it dawned that his being on this road was no coincidence—that he had obviously come out to look for her. 'Anyway, Clem didn't actually *tell* me not to take it out. He just said it was—— Oh, I don't know! I just thought he thought I wasn't that experienced a rider. I'd hardly have been crazy enough to risk breaking my neck if I'd known how spirited he was!'

'No?' From the sceptical lift of an eyebrow, clearly he thought she was. 'You're one hell of an insurance risk, lady——' and stabbing a finger at his chest '—with me as the potential loser. You're about the most irresponsible individual I've ever come across—and believe me I've met a few! If you can't have any respect for your own safety, just try and consider other people's! There's no end of damage that animal might have done—to itself, others, not to mention property!—through your thoughtless, unerring need to give in to those reckless whims! If you were more than a mere guest in my house, instead of some crazy-minded, mixed-up American, I'd——'

'You'd what?' Sasha challenged, sticking her chin in the air. How could he keep on at her like this when she had already said she was sorry?

'What are you asking for—a demonstration?'

She had never seen such angry purpose in a man's eyes before, her breathed, 'Oh, for heaven's sake!' with her hasty attempt to get out of the car followed by a small cry as an emotion—hot as molten iron—precipitated the swift, painful lock of his fingers around her arm.

'Yes, *for heaven's sake*!' His face was scored with fury and the muscles were clenched tight on either side of his jaw. 'What sort of mentality is there to a woman who can't see the danger in climbing out on to broken window-ledges? Riding horses she'd been warned not to ride? Accepting lifts from just anyone? For goodness' sake! Is life so cheap?'

'*Yes*!' She flung it at him with all the anguish that was in her heart and she saw hard puzzlement cross his face, then a sudden, dawning comprehension.

Slowly, he scanned the tormented lines of her face, those grey eyes too keen, too discerning, and amazingly, as if someone had already told him, he said in a quietly coaxing tone, 'What happened to him? What happened, Sasha?'

It was a long time since she had spoken about it to anyone. Even her parents had come to respect her reticence and didn't talk about it any more. But Rex had somehow found the flaw in her protective armour—broken through the barriers of her defence—and all her pain and months of silent guilt came pouring out of her, undeterred now.

'We were getting married,' she said, with a suffocating lump pressing against her windpipe. 'I'd known him since college—he was my art tutor—and we'd been waiting until I'd established myself in my career before settling down. Then ten days before the wedding—I suddenly felt so unsure. Ben said it was pre-wedding nerves and that he'd gone through the same thing a couple of weeks before—and I believed him. When he collapsed the next day they thought it was through overworking and that he'd be all right—only he wasn't. They said he'd had something wrong with his heart—but really it was all my fault.'

She hadn't cried in a long time—not properly—but now the tears came unchecked, slowly and silently at first, and then in hard, convulsive sobs, and she didn't care any more what Rex thought about her, not even aware at first of being drawn against him, or that that broad shoulder was taking all the brunt of her emotion.

He didn't say anything at all, just let her cry until her sobs subsided and then he didn't release her immediately so that gradually she became more aware of things, like his steady breathing, like the tang of his aftershave, and the fact that that impeccable shoulder she had been leaning on was now quite damp from her tears.

'If he had what they said he did,' suddenly he was saying softly, 'it would have happened anyway— sooner or later. Maybe he *had* been overworking—or maybe it was just all too much excitement with the wedding—but it certainly wasn't your fault. And what you were suffering from was cold feet—it's a common but temporary symptom experienced by a lot of engaged couples. In fact I have a couple of friends who each went through a period of uncertainty just before the due date and who have been happily married to each other with an ever-increasing brood for the past fifteen years. Stop punishing yourself,' he advised with both warmth and understanding in his voice.

His lips brushed her temple and she sucked in her breath, inhaling that subtle, fresh scent of him that was pleasingly male. He was stronger than she was. Even unable to walk, he was stronger, emotionally, than any man she had ever met, and unconsciously she clutched at the soft cloth of his sleeves, drawing something vital from the comfort of his hard warmth.

Suddenly, though, he was looking past her with those black brows drawn together and she knew, even without turning round, that Clem was coming back.

'Here,' he said gently, handing her a clean white handkerchief, and though he had released her she was aware of a protective arm still lying across her shoulders as, gratefully, she blew her nose.

Clem looked smug, she thought, catching the glance he sent her as he got into the car, probably deducing from the little scene he saw in the back that his employer had quite rightly subjected her to a verbal flaying and was now kissing away the invisible weals.

'Thank you, Clem.' There was authority in that simple yet meaningful comment by Rex, all it took for the chauffeur hastily to discard the ostensibly needed newspaper and start the car without a word.

CHAPTER FIVE

HELPING Sheila dead-head the blooms in the rose garden beyond the front terrace, Sasha inhaled the delicate perfume of the buds she had also helped gather, preparing to start back to the house.

'I suppose you're getting stuck into your painting again this morning,' Rex's mother remarked as Sasha stopped to retrieve a whisper of decorative fennel the other woman had dropped.

'No, she isn't.' Both women looked up, surprised by the intrusive yet determined masculine voice drifting across the terrace. 'She's been working hard enough of late and she's taking some time off—as of now!'

'Oh, am I?' Though her eyes glittered defiantly, Sasha's words were injected with a little tremor. In a black T-shirt and jeans, Rex looked incredible! she thought, distractedly aware of the way the muscles bulged in his arms as he manoeuvred his chair over the flagstones.

'Oh, well . . .' Clearly sensing the tension between Sasha and her son, Sheila pulled a wry face—a look that told Sasha she hadn't a chance of winning— before hurrying off with the obvious excuse of having to see Dee.

'How are you this morning?' Over the tap of his mother's retreating footsteps, Rex spoke with a gentle concern.

'I'm fine,' Sasha smiled, and seeing those grey eyes narrow, 'I am—really,' she stressed, her gaze embracing the fertile garden, the clear blue of the sky. It had been misty earlier, but now the sun was shining brilliantly, combining with the late summer dew to make everything sparkle, seem fresh and sweet and alive.

'You've been under one hell of a lot of strain since you've been here,' he remarked, so that she wasn't sure whether he was referring to her losing her passport, her money and everything, or to the things she had told him yesterday in the car. But he had handled her gently ever since, his wise and solicitous suggestion last night that she have a warm bath to soothe the bruises she had only then realised she had acquired from being thrown, that she'd feel better after an early night, proving to be right, because she did, feeling her argumentative spirits coming to the fore again as he reminded her, 'You were only in this country a few days before you landed yourself in the fix you're in now—and you told me yourself you haven't seen much of anything besides London and the coast—so you're going to take a break and start doing what you came here to do—and that's enjoy yourself.'

'But I am enjoying myself!'

'Nevertheless . . .' His tone was conclusive as his gaze shifted from the slim hand clutching the roses to her sleek black hair, to the unadorned simplicity of her features. 'We're going to do some sightseeing today so go and get yourself ready.'

He was going to take her? Ignoring the warm tide of excitement pulsing through her, Sasha hastened to comply, substituting her shorts and T-shirt for some calf-length white leggings, a bronze silk shirt and matching sandals.

'Very impressive.' Rex's grin was wolfish as she joined him in the back of the BMW, and Sasha felt her colour rising from that lazy gaze travelling over her.

What was he referring to? Her appearance? she wondered hectically. Or to the little time she'd taken getting ready? She'd been determined not to keep him waiting, though, and she could only hope he hadn't guessed at how eager she'd been to spend the day with him as she heard Clem close her door, get into the car.

The day out comprised an unhurried tour of most of Constable country, with a visit initially to the site of the artist's famous *Hay Wain*—Flatford Mill.

'Apart from those extra trees it's almost exactly as it was when Constable painted it,' Sasha commented delightedly from the riverbank, happy to see that the famous cottage in his painting had been preserved by the National Trust and that the land beyond the trees on the other side of the river and the red brick mill-house was as natural and undeveloped as it had been in the great man's time.

'I think he might have had something to say about all these tourists.' Rex winked up at her in a way that made Sasha's stomach do a double flip. And it wasn't just her he was affecting!

Strolling beside him while he used that superb physical strength to manoeuvre himself around—because he wouldn't let her help him—Sasha was amazed at the degree of female interest he was attracting. They were practically falling over themselves for a chance to do something for him! she thought wryly, wondering how much it had to do with the wheelchair or with those compellingly masculine good looks.

He was certainly right about one thing, though, she thought, looking around. The place was alive with visitors.

Budding artists sat sketching outside the beautifully preserved cottage. The tea-shop overlooking the river was doing a good trade, and the tiny bridge leading to the fields across the water was teeming with tourists, some hiring boats, or doing the charted walks, others simply standing, admiring the tranquil views.

'Would you mind if I took one last photograph?'

They were on their way back to the car park, just passing the bridge, and Sasha's heart fluttered as Rex smiled indulgently up at her. 'No, go ahead.'

She hurried off, up on to the bridge, getting a wide-angle shot across the fields. Then, coming back to the path to join him, she stopped dead in her tracks.

A huge, hairy wolfhound had two paws on Rex's chair, tail wagging as it lavished him with unwanted affection. Rex was laughing as he tried to avoid the friendly tongue, laughing up at the pretty young woman who was trying to drag the dog away.

'I really am sorry about this,' Sasha heard her apologising as she approached them, 'but he isn't always so disobedient. You must have a way with dogs for him to do that. But your jeans...I really am sorry...' The dog had obviously been in the river and now Sasha could see the muddy prints on the denim covering one of those long, lean thighs. 'Are you sure I couldn't give you something towards the cost of cleaning? Or is there anything else I could do...?'

Why don't you take them off and wash them for him? Sasha had to bite her tongue to stop herself saying, not sure who was slobbering over him most, the dog or its owner.

'Oh...I'm sorry.' Suddenly aware of Sasha, the girl was looking her up and down as though wondering what she was doing with such a sexy-looking hunk as, somehow, she managed to bring her dog under control.

'That's all right—don't worry about it.' Rex's smile would have liquefied silver, Sasha decided wryly, seeing the other girl's melting response before she dragged herself and the wolfhound reluctantly away.

'I can't leave you for five minutes, can I?' she chided laughingly. 'Are you sure you wouldn't rather I went away again to save me cramping your style?'

Brushing his muddy leg, Rex was looking at her obliquely. 'Now why do I get the feeling that you don't really mean that?' he drawled, amused.

Sasha felt that unbidden chemistry tug at her senses. '*I* don't mind,' she attempted nonchalantly. So why did it have to come out sounding as though she did? 'Does it happen everywhere you go—all this unwarranted attention?'

'Why? Feeling left out?' he teased as they started moving on again. 'Perhaps you should get one of these.' He gestured down at his chair, for once making light of it. 'You'd be surprised at the different concept of life one gets purely from this level.'

'I'll bet I would!' She laughed drily, her swinging hair dark and sleek above the bronze silk. 'For a start it seems to provoke a fatal attraction in dogs and cats!'

He laughed, loudly and genuinely, amusement softening his features. 'They probably just fancy the prospect of a permanent lap!'

'*They*? Or their owners?' Sasha remarked with a grimace. She knew one young woman who would have been on his knee without any persuasion if he'd given her the chance!

'Ooh . . . nasty!' Rex sent a mock-reproving glance in her direction. 'Now what would provoke such a waspish reaction like that, I wonder?'

Those teasing eyes were too shrewd and a little breathlessly she laughed, 'Oh, the masculine ego!' And, noticing that the small slope to the car park—specially provided for the disabled—was proving hard work even for him, she added with deliberate impudence, 'I'll fetch your servant, sir,' and felt a reckless thrill from the look he shot her as she hurried off to get Clem.

After that the day just seemed to grow more and more enjoyable, probably because Rex was determined that she shouldn't miss anything he felt she should have seen. He seemed to share a genuine interest in Constable's works too, she thought, feeling sure he wasn't just indulging her when, having instructed Clem to stop in a lay-by only minutes after leaving the car park, he glanced up from the picture postcard she'd bought and was still admiring of the famous *Cornfield*, and said, 'There you are—just for you, Sasha—the real thing.'

High on a hill, they were looking out across the peaceful panorama of Dedham Vale: lush green meadows, copsed by secretive woods and crossed by streams; the grey tower of Dedham Church creating a timeless landmark, as unobtrusive as the meandering river and the trees. A lane stole sharply downwards from the road. She could see it dropping at a right angle to it on the left of the magnificent view. The lane on her postcard? she struggled hopefully to recognise, her gaze returning constantly to the blazing gold of swaying corn—a whole field of it!—right in front of them, sloping towards the contrasting green of the valley.

'Is that it . . . ?' Common sense told her it couldn't possibly be. There were too many discrepancies, and yet . . .

Rex laughed, leaning across to look at the little card she was holding, making her disturbingly conscious of that arm across the back of her seat. 'Have you found it?' he queried, amused.

'Well, I think so . . .' With a wave of heat across her skin owing more to that arm than the mellow sunshine, she studied the sweeping landscape. 'But then if it were . . . the church wouldn't be in the right place . . .'

Rex's laughter stirred her hair with its gentle warmth. 'Artist's licence,' he informed her smilingly. 'I'm sure you know all about that! It's a fact Constable used it to get the best out of his work—as with that one,' he said with a jerk of his chin towards her postcard, 'but the cold reality behind that particular painting is that he couldn't sell it for ten years.'

'Ten *years*?' Amazed, Sasha looked down at the little card to the cleverly depicted gold of the ripe corn, to the movement in the sheltering trees and the stream where the little boy was drinking—the feeling in the whole composition—and her heart went out to the English artist. 'It must have broken his heart,' she murmured sadly.

Rex shrugged. 'I don't think so. He just went on painting,' he said. 'One doesn't quit just because things don't work out as one plans initially. That's the difference between making it and not making it— determination. Not to be beaten by setbacks. To keep trying. It's called resilience,' he stated matter-of-factly.

And he had it, she thought, knowing instinctively that he was made of the same grit. In which case, why did he spurn all the people who were trying to help him? The very people who might have helped him to walk?

The eyes she lifted to his were soft and limpid with a deep need to understand him, and she saw the glint of some answering emotion flare in his. Desire, she thought, swallowing, feeling that sudden sweet tightening in her stomach, and she knew that if the other man hadn't been there then he would have kissed her. Thank heaven for Clem! she thought, confused.

She was still struggling to come to terms with the way she was feeling as they came through one of the picturesque villages, and beside her she heard Rex say, 'This is Kersey. It's earned the name from some as the prettiest village in England.'

And she could see why. Sloping steeply upwards, the main street was a hotchpotch of timber-framed buildings jostling beside pretty pink-washed cottages and larger, elegant houses where the more prosperous past-century merchants must have lived. They had made their wealth from the wool trade that had prevailed in East Anglia in days long gone, she remembered reading, and the labour provided by their poorer neighbours, but the focal point of the village, she decided, looking around, was the little ford which divided it in two.

'Oh, how quaint!' She couldn't help laughing as she read the small sign advising 'Give Way to Ducks', and as the BMW slowed down she leaned forward, aware of Rex's warm smile as she watched a plump white bird waddle through the water-splash in front of them. 'I could see us doing *that* in New York!'

'Do you like living in such a big city?' His tone implied that, in spite of the thriving empire he controlled in the very pulse of his own country, he preferred the country himself—as his home would testify. 'You don't exactly strike me as the type of girl who'd be that happy out of an entirely rural location—and with your type of work I'd imagine you could live anywhere. So why New York?'

Sasha shrugged. 'Habit, I suppose—I've always lived there, although both my parents invited me to go with them when they married again.'

'Why didn't you?' There was a curious hesitation in his voice as though he realised he might be treading on private ground, although, strangely, she found she could talk about it more painlessly now.

'Ben's work was in New York and I wanted to stay nearer him. Since he died...' She shrugged again rather aimlessly. 'I don't know...'

'You said he was your tutor?' Rex pressed quietly, reminding her of what she'd told him the day before.

'Yes, though I'd known him since high school—when he came to live in our district. He was a really marvellous teacher,' she said, smilingly. 'Sometimes I think he taught me everything I know.' They had been attracted to each other from the start, but it hadn't been a dangerous attraction producing the type of heated excitement in her that she'd experienced so unwillingly when the man sitting beside her had taken her in his arms. With Ben it had just started quietly—and grown into a comfortable warmth.

And, as though Rex had followed her train of thoughts, in a voice low enough so as not to be heard in the front he asked sombrely, 'Were you living together?' It wasn't meant in any detrimental or inquisitive way; just an understanding of how much more devastating things could have been for her if they had been.

'No,' she said flatly, though they had been occasional lovers. In fact, at the time, and sometimes since, looking back, she'd wondered why he hadn't wanted her more. 'My parents are rather old-fashioned and wouldn't have liked it,' she went on, feeling rather sheepish admitting, 'And I didn't want to do anything to upset them. We were going to live in my apartment as soon as we were married and now...' She made a small, futile gesture with her hand. 'I don't know. The prospect of living in the country is becoming more and more attractive, so maybe one day I'll move to New England—nearer Dad.'

That male mouth quirked in silent contemplation and then unexpectedly he reached across and took her hand, causing her breath to lock.

'I'm afraid I can't offer you New England.' She could tell that he was smiling, though she was looking down at those long, tanned fingers entwined with hers. 'But what about a real *old* English tea?'

Consequently, that was how she found herself, twenty minutes later, sitting beside him in the tiny cottage-café, tucking into home-made scones with lashings of jam and thick, whipped cream.

'How long has Clem worked for you?' she asked about the man who, whether at Rex's dismissal or out

of some code of unspoken discretion, hadn't joined
them for afternoon tea.

'He started as my father's stablehand when he was
just a lad and has been at the Halt ever since. He'll
tackle anything, and he's fiercely loyal to his job—
and to me and my family—second only to his own.'

'He's married?' Sasha breathed, amazed, cutting
through the fluffy white mound of her scone.

'Hardly.' Rex's grimace assured her that such a
possibility was as unlikely as she'd imagined it to be.
'I mean family of the maternal and fraternal kind.
Clem's a man's man. I'm afraid he doesn't have a
great deal of time for women.' Was he telling her!
'Probably because the woman he chose ran off and
married someone else and I think that nowadays he
sees the female sex as rather a threat to his very safe
and comfortable existence.'

'Like me?' Sasha suggested, before she could stop
herself, having felt at times that Clem Baldwin regarded her as a definite interloper between him and
his adored employer. But the significance of what she
had said suddenly struck her, making her cheeks burn
with colour so that quickly she bit into the cool cream
of her scone, hoping that Rex wouldn't notice.

'We've all been turned upside-down by you, Sasha,'
he said softly, with an almost sensual amusement in
his eyes, and she looked down at the dark liquid fruit
of the jam he was applying liberally to a layer of
equally thick cream, wondering exactly what he had
meant by that. Had she affected *him* that much?

'I guess I cause chaos everywhere I go,' she laughed,
trying to shrug off the strangely weakening effects of
his remark. Then, in an effort to change the subject,
'And you're supposed to spread the cream on top of

the jam—not the other way round.' At least, that was what her English grandmother used to say.

He laughed with her as he bit into the sinful-looking half-scone with an appreciative masculine appetite. 'Uh-uh.' Amused, he was shaking his head, licking jam from the dark olive of a finger. 'Cream first— jam afterwards. The cream replaces the butter. Anyone who's anyone knows that—though I must admit opinion on that point differs enough to start a second civil war. What will you be—a roundhead or a royalist? If I were you I'd go for the royalist. You look positively fetching with that white moustache.'

'Ooh!' Quickly, Sasha wiped her mouth with the pretty paper napkin, responding to his teasing smile as he stirred milk into his tea. 'Just because your mouth's big enough to cram everything in at once,' she joked, enjoying this light banter with him. 'That better?' Tilting her head back for his inspection, she was totally unprepared for the way he suddenly leaned forward and, catching her chin, brushed the corner of her mouth lightly with his.

'Infinitely,' he breathed, and sat back again, leaving her senses clinging to that tantalising masculine scent, his intimate warmth, the sensuality behind that seemingly innocent kiss. 'And if you don't want to evoke responses like that, don't provoke them,' he advised on a strangely uneven note that belied the casual ease of his smile.

'I wasn't.' Was she? she puzzled, knowing that if his voice had been unsteady, then hers would have topped the limit on the Richter scale! And, aghast that he might possibly think she'd been openly flirting with him, she sent a deliberate glance around at the cleverly plaited straw shapes of handbells, horns and horseshoes decorating the walls of the little café and which she'd seen on the counter for sale, and with a calm she was far from feeling changed course by remarking, 'What a cute name—corn dollies. Why do they call them that?'

From the knowing look he gave her, he knew why she had changed the subject, but with a cursory glance at the wall beside their table he gave her a wry smile and said, 'It means dolly as in icon or idol. A throwback from pagan days. Nowadays dolly making's just become a hobby—something to tempt the tourists with—but at one time it was a very essential part of English country life. The dolly was made from the last handfuls of corn and was a kind of symbol of thanks to the gods for a good harvest, although views clashed about what the dolly actually represented. Some believed it had to be trampled into the ground to destroy any evil spirits that might be lurking in the corn. Others regarded it as an emblem of fertility. Some believed that that last cutting contained the corn spirit who'd retreated into it when the rest of the crop had been harvested. She was supposed to sleep in the dolly during the winter months, waiting for spring when her refuge would be taken back to the fields where the new seed was being sown. The story is that there she'd slip, unnoticed, into the newly sown crop and bring it to life.'

There was something about the way he said it that conjured up all the magical romance of that bygone age, and she uttered a small sigh. 'I like that version best,' she whispered.

His smile was almost smug. 'I thought you would,' he said. But it was the way he was looking at her with those disturbingly perceptive eyes that caused a tightness in her throat, made her heart beat a little too quickly as he took control of the conversation, forcing it back to things she didn't want to face, by saying, 'And if you want to know why I'm finding it immensely difficult keeping my hands off you, it's quite simply because you're—if you'll excuse the simile—like freshly baked bread to a man who's been constantly fed a diet of rich, fancy cakes.'

There was a tremor in her laugh. 'You mean plain, white and crusty?' she uttered in self-mockery, every nerve trembling in response to what he had just said, making it hard to meet those comparatively serious grey eyes.

'I mean full of substance, naturally lovely and with more than just a promise of being wholly satisfying to a man—and because we both know that we'd be lying to deny that there's a degree of physical attraction between us—— No, not a degree, dammit, a full-blown chemistry that in other circumstances would have produced one hell of an explosion by now! But you're not ready for a serious relationship yet, Sasha, and I'm not the man—even if you were—who's able to give you one. Oh, I don't mean we couldn't have a relationship at its most basic level, but where I'm concerned there are other things to consider...'

Like Lorraine? She didn't know why the name of his lovely cousin should surface above everything else. He meant nothing to her, Sasha, after all.

'You were right first time—I'm nowhere near ready,' she breathed in an emphatic attempt to deny—to herself as much as anyone else—that all he would have to do would be to take her in his arms and Ben would be—— She cut the thought dead, and in a tight little voice uttered, 'So you see, you've got nothing to fear.

I'm not looking for a relationship with any man right now. And anyway...' for some reason she had to say it '...I was under the impression you were pretty heavily committed to Lorraine.'

'Oh, were you?' The high arching of an eyebrow was almost a reprimand—almost as though he objected to his cousin being discussed. 'And what—or who—gave you that idea?'

Sasha swallowed. She couldn't say, Dee did; not to mention Lorraine's own obviousness that said more than any words could possibly have done. 'Aren't you?' she parried, with a twist of some indefinable emotion.

For a moment those grey eyes seemed to bore right through her, only the suggestion of some dark, personal conflict giving any life to his expression.

'How can I possibly marry Lorraine—or any woman—like this?' he growled, his mouth twisting savagely as he sent a downward glance towards the inescapable prison of his chair.

'I'm sorry.' She didn't know what else to say, her face lined with understanding of his pain and frustration, while her own emotions felt as bruised and vulnerable as the trampled corn to which he had been referring. Then, 'You might not always be——'

'Forget it,' he snarled, scything her sentence short. 'I've already told you—I don't need your pity.' And tossing a glance at her plate and her half-eaten scone, 'Have you finished?' he was suddenly demanding with harsh impatience.

If she hadn't, she had now, she thought, feeling her appetite desert her like the fleeing corn spirit, along with the light mood of the afternoon.

'I didn't mean it like that.' Able-bodied as she was, she had a job keeping up with him as he engaged that leashed energy to propel himself towards the counter, the business of settling the bill, which earned him a slavish smile from the young female cashier, Sasha noted with some resentment, thwarting her immediate attempt to make amends.

'You know I didn't mean it like that,' she reiterated as, despite his brooding mood, he still retained enough cool courtesy to allow her to precede him out into the mellow stillness of the afternoon.

The tea-shop was in a village high street, but Clem hadn't yet come back with the car, and so she sank down on to the low wall that fronted the shop, appreciative of the sun's warmth on her face and bare arms, instilling her with the courage to say, 'I know you can't walk, but sometimes, Rex, you're impossible! Sometimes you're just too plain touchy about it for words!'

And he could throw her out of his house if he decided to! Which he probably would, she thought hopelessly, judging by the way his eyes were suddenly dissecting her.

It was a complete shock, therefore, when that rigid male mouth pulled in a softening grimace and he said, 'So now I've been a total heel and reduced you to tears again.'

Which was almost true—but not quite.

'I'm not crying.' Defiantly, she stuck her nose in the air because she felt surprisingly close to it, staring sightlessly at the little latticed panes of the tearoom so that she felt a shock like an electric current run through her as he suddenly caught her hand and pressed it to his lips.

'Pity,' he breathed in a voice as soft as velvet. 'At least I could handle that.'

But she couldn't! she thought wildly, closing her eyes, every nerve-end throbbing as those warm lips moved to the wildly leaping pulse in her wrist, every feminine cell crying out in recognition of the elemental need which trembled through her.

She'd agreed with him that she wasn't ready for a relationship, but she was! And with him! she was forced to acknowledge now, the moist heat of his tongue on the tender inside of her arm widening that chasm of need inside of her that ached to be fulfilled.

She was breathing shallowly, the distant hum of a car engine and the light chink-chink of crockery from the tea-shop sounds lost beneath a tide of sweet sensation as desire, stronger than any she had known, licked like an uncontrolled flame along her veins. She felt the tingling in her breasts as they flowered beneath the soft fabric of her shirt, felt the pangs of a healthy sexual hunger, suddenly fully awakened and all the more intense for the long, empty months of self-denial.

'God!' That raw, masculine emotion forced her lids apart. Rex had lifted his head, and a bright incandescent heat burned in his eyes. 'You make me feel things I've got no right to feel, Sasha,' he breathed huskily. No right, she guessed, not so much because of that accident that had left him paralysed but, she thought, with a deep, inexplicable emotion, because of Lorraine.

'It's just as well, then, that you're about to be saved,' she murmured, tremulous from the touch of those cool fingers—still lingering on her skin—and the enervating emotions that gave a sexy huskiness to her voice, so that she was more than relieved to see the BMW pulling up beside them.

CHAPTER SIX

THE days seemed to tumble into each other, Sasha marvelled, working out that she had been at the Halt for almost three weeks, and in England almost four.

She still hadn't had any luck in contacting her mother. Any day now, though, she knew that Susan and Cyrus Conway would have to return home and then, when she'd got her own finances sorted out—finished her fresco—she realised with a swift, piercing ache inside that there would be nothing to keep her there. Until then, though, she thought, she would be grateful for every day she could spend at the Halt, and even more for the evenings when each night after dinner Sheila Templeton would slip away to check on the horses, or to catch up with the paperwork for the various charitable organisations she was involved with, and she, Sasha, would be left alone with Rex.

It was these nights that she most looked forward to, and the long, intellectual and equally light-hearted conversations with him that sometimes lasted way into the early hours.

She had never enjoyed talking—or listening—to anyone so much, and quite simply it was a wrench to drag herself out of his company and off to bed at night. But there was always an unspoken signal, a look, a laugh, or even a sigh, a mutual, silent communication of an ever-present sexual awareness that day by day was threatening to flare into life. And she knew that one day, if she ignored that signal and stayed, then that iron restraint of Rex's would snap, the talking would stop, and she'd find herself involved in an affair with a man who was already halfway committed to someone else—an affair she neither wanted nor would be able to control.

Strangely, though, the urge to write which she'd thought had died with Ben had suddenly returned in force, and she found herself with a new idea for one of her little books. The last one had failed, she knew now, because the rag doll theme she'd used had remained limp and lifeless, merely symbolising the way she'd been feeling herself. Even so, the result of her new motivation startled her as, under the skill of her pencil, a little straw dolly came to life.

The spirit of the Suffolk countryside had filled her with inspiration, she told herself flippantly, given her creative processes new vitality, just as the legendary corn spirit breathed new life into the corn. But deep down she knew it wasn't only that. She was reaping her inspiration from something more than just the lovely environment, something that was too new and too dangerous fully to acknowledge—even to herself. But the days were no longer hours just to get through. She was feeling good just being alive. And only Gavin Chase attempted to put the damper on her spirts, like the evening she went swimming with him in town.

'What do you mean you can't see me for lunch because you're seeing Rex Templeton?' Pulling himself out of the pool, Gavin followed her across the wet, tiled floor, sounding unduly irate against the echoing splashes and shrieks of the public baths. 'Since when?' Wet fingers clutched her arm, preventing her from rushing off into the changing-room. Clearly, he wasn't happy about her plans for the following day. 'You aren't getting yourself involved with him, are you? You'll only be making a fool of yourself if you are. It's common knowledge his beautiful cousin's the red-hot favourite—and the only reason he doesn't tie the knot with her is...' His gaze drifted down over her gentle curves beneath the blue satin swimsuit. 'Well...you know how he is.'

Not inclined to discuss her reasons for seeing Rex, or to talk about Lorraine Faraday, Sasha, tight-lipped, tried to pull away. But Gavin didn't let her, determined to continue. 'Apparently, he was dead serious about someone he was seeing for more than four years before the accident, but it seems she left him for a job abroad when she was told he probably wouldn't walk again. The lovely Lorraine was waiting—willing and eager—to pick up the pieces—and you don't come between a cosy little familial bonding like that.'

'Who says I'm trying to?' Determinedly, Sasha pulled free of his restraining hand. 'Poor Rex,' she breathed almost to herself, shuddering from more than just the cold water running down over her shoulders from her dripping hair. How could any woman have been that cruel?

'He's hardly that, is he?' said Gavin drily—in rather bad taste, Sasha thought—before he went on, 'But I agree, she must have been one hell of a bitch. But that doesn't give him the right to try and steal my girl's affections when he's more than adequately provided for as it is. And if you're around—shopping in London tomorrow lunchtime—you can come up to my office, not his.'

'No, I can't, Gavin.' Momentarily, she was distracted by the sudden loud splashes of three teenage boys diving off the side into the pool. 'When I make promises I keep them,' she said, unpretentiously acquainting him with just one of the simple standards she set herself to live by, while a little guiltily remembering her breathless response to Rex's invitation that morning—like a teenager accepting her first date. 'And you might think I'm your girl...' she hugged herself as she started to shiver '...but if I stay here talking to you much longer I'll just be some poor unfortunate soul with pneumonia!' She laughed, wondering if he'd guess the reason for that unusual lightness in her stride as she turned away, towards the changing-rooms.

She took the train up to London the following morning and spent a couple of hours ambling around the busy Oxford Street shops. Consequently, when she arrived at the large Templeton Technics building, she was loaded up with an assortment of bags.

'Hello, Sasha. You look as though you've had a good morning.' Coming out of the office where her employer was evidently speaking on the telephone, Dee was her usual friendly self. 'Like a coffee while you're waiting?' Rex's voice was muffled by the door closing behind her, but just the sound of those deep tones had been enough to make excitement curl in Sasha's stomach, and at that moment she didn't think she could have eaten or drunk a thing.

'No, thanks, Dee. I'll wait till lunchtime.' From one of the plush couches that lined the outer office, she smiled up at the older woman, her mouth tinged with a creamy pink lipstick. It was the only make-up she was wearing and which she'd taken care to reapply in the ladies' room of the last store she'd visited, because she wanted to look her best. But now, considering Dee's immaculate suit and blouse, a look that

mirrored the high-heeled elegance of the chic receptionist who had shown her up there, Sasha was beginning to feel totally unsophisticated in her sleeveless
white top, her full blue cotton skirt and sandals.

'Is she disrupting my office already, Dee?' There
was dry amusement in the commanding voice coming
over the intercom. 'Send her in before the place comes
to a total standstill.'

'Just remind him he hasn't got you working for him
yet. At least, not on his office payroll!' Dee joked,
her laughing grimace informing Sasha of the obvious
repartee that existed between Rex and his staff, and
also of the respect he would command as Dee showed
her into his office.

'Good morning.' He viewed her appreciatively from
behind the large mahogany desk, and Sasha's pulse
raced. In an impeccable dark suit he looked every bit
the king in a commercial jungle—ruthless and
dangerous—that undeniable authority only tempered
by the burnished sensuality of his smile.

'It's afternoon,' Sasha corrected, and felt a swift
dart of satisfaction in contradicting him, which he was
fully aware of, she realised from the subtle movement
of an eyebrow, before he dropped a glance to the gold
watch on his wrist and said smoothly,

'So it is.' Casually he was examining the various
bags she was carrying. 'What have you been buying?
All of Oxford Street by the look of it.'

She laughed, but surprisingly he seemed genuinely
interested as he gestured for her to sit down, and from
the chair opposite his she shrugged, and with a glance
down at the purchases she'd dropped down beside her
chair said, 'Only some new casual things I can feel

comfortable enough to paint in, some new brushes, a sketchpad . . .'

'What *else*?' She looked up, hearing him laughing softly. 'No designer dresses? No glittering jewellery? No exotic perfume?' Amusement lingered on his lips as he made an unsettling study of her complexion, of her dark, unplucked brows and the velvety black lashes that were thick and long enough not to warrant mascara, and some mysterious emotion seemed to stir in his eyes.

'No,' she said, peeved that he might be comparing her lack of style with the chic women in his office—with Lorraine. 'I'm not particularly interested in things like that.'

'No,' was all he said in flat agreement, so that she couldn't tell whether he disapproved or not. Then, 'I spoke to my mother on the phone this morning. She told me you finished the fresco last night.'

Somewhat startled by his abrupt change of topic, Sasha responded with a simple, 'Yes.' She had completed it after she had returned from the baths with Gavin—working late, but Rex hadn't come in at all last night, as far as she knew, and with a dull ache somewhere below her ribcage she wondered if he had been with Lorraine.

'Good,' he said succinctly, satisfaction etching his features as he sat back, clasping his hands behind his head. The fine shirt pulled against those powerful muscles, barely concealing the dark olive of his chest beneath.

Sasha swallowed. Like that, it was difficult to remember he was in a wheelchair. 'You haven't seen it finished. You might not like it,' she said, touching her tongue to her top lip with a small nervous gesture.

'That's right.' He was doing it deliberately, she felt—to assess her reactions—holding her gaze with such a shrewed calculation that she was forced to lower hers. 'I might decide it's not what I wanted at all—and then you'll really be in my debt, won't you, Sasha?' He was joking, of course, but in a tone so sensually provoking that, with a dryness in her throat, she watched the movements of those tanned, lean hands as they gathered up various papers. Competent, virile hands, she thought, wondering what it would be like to feel their hair-silkened touch against her cheek, against the fevered satin of her skin...

'Now what would you like to do?'

Quickly, Sasha looked up from the file he was closing, blushing as profusely as if he had read her thoughts.

'Do?' she uttered with a painful contraction of her throat. Wasn't he simply taking her to lunch?

'Yes, *do*,' he emphasised, a little impatiently. 'Even you couldn't have seen all of London in the short time you've been here. So where would you like to go?'

'I—I don't know,' she stammered over her heart's sudden, ridiculous hammering. 'You choose.'

So he did, first authorising Clem to take them to the restaurant he had booked earlier, where, on a sunny balcony, overlooking the Thames, they ate fresh langoustine salads with warm, crusty bread and white wine. And alone—because, as usual, Clem had made himself scarce—they watched the barges and pleasure boats cutting through the sun-streaked water, while Rex acquainted her with the names of the busy bridges that joined the south side of the city with the north.

'You Americans claimed our old London Bridge for yourselves...' his eyes glittered warmly over the pink flesh of the langoustine he was tearing into '...so I'm afraid you'll have to go to Arizona to see that.'

Sasha's hand flew to her chest in feigned disappointment. 'And I came all this way to see it, too! These Americans take everything!' She giggled, picking up her glass, taking a long draught of her wine. It was a Chardonnay—crisp and cold and delicious. 'Are you objecting?' she queried lightly, her dark hair stirring in the gentle breeze.

'Not at the moment.' He gave her a lop-sided grin. 'After all, we've got you.'

Sasha stared down at the pale gold of her wine. 'Hardly the best compensation for a bridge,' she uttered with laughter in her voice, its tremor lost beneath the sudden blast of a boat's horn a little way upriver.

'It depends whose standpoint you're looking from.'

He was only flirting with her, she knew. So why let such skilled dalliance start her blood surging through her veins? After all, she wasn't a teenager, and it wasn't as if she weren't used to men flirting with her. But then never before had she met a man with the type of magnetism that Rex Templeton positively oozed, and which disturbed her so much—and not least, she thought, because she felt such a powerful response to it.

She murmured some light, inane comment, not sure how to cope, and across the table heard him—aware—say, 'You know, for a twenty-six year old who's also been engaged, you seem refreshingly but surprisingly naïve.'

'And you,' she laughed, trying to appear blasé, despite the colour she could feel staining her cheeks, 'are an outrageous flirt!'

'No,' he stated quietly, his gaze falling to the ivory column of her throat, the soft rise of her breasts beneath the cotton top. 'I just appreciate beautiful, things.'

The sensuality in his voice took Sasha's breath away. The breeze was teasing his hair, lifting the sleek black strands, the bright sunlight magnifying the sheer force and vitality in those handsome features, so that, trapped by that grey gaze, her throat clogging with sensation, before she knew it she was murmuring, 'So do I.'

He smiled, a slow, sensual smile, a tension so terrifyingly strong crackling between them that Sasha grabbed at any straw to try and restore some level of normality to her senses, saying quickly, tremulously, 'What did you have in mind to do this afternoon?'

As he tossed down his serviette, Rex's smile was purely vulpine now, although there was a husky quality to his voice when he answered, 'Besides a strong desire to take you home and make love to you, I thought we might do the National Gallery next.'

And there was no answer to that, so she didn't even attempt to offer one—couldn't have because of the way her heart was pounding—as Rex, after ascertaining that she had had enough to eat, rang Clem on the portable phone he carried in his briefcase and summoned the waiter for the bill.

Time passed on wings that afternoon, and though they had to use the rear entrance of the gallery to accommodate Rex's chair Sasha couldn't help marvelling at the sheer determination with which he overcame his immobility to accompany her, share her appreciation of the paintings.

'Look at that vitality and life...' Her words tailed off as she stood face to face with Constable's famous *Hay Wain*, her artistic eye appreciating his clever use of colour, the splashes of red and brilliant white that were his trademark in such contrast to the gentler, natural tones he'd used in this, his most renowned work. 'I can't believe I'm seeing this...'

She could have stayed looking at that painting forever. It was something she had seen on countless calendars, prints and postcards, yet nothing could compare with the reality of genius—face to face. It was her first visit to that particular gallery too, and, though she hadn't expressed her surprise openly to Rex for remembering that, she was, however, grateful to him for bringing her there. And transfixed, suddenly aware of him sitting there beside her, she murmured, 'I'm sorry. I—I can't leave yet. Do you mind?'

'Take all the time you need.' His smile was indulgent, those deep tones warm and understanding. No other man would have been as patient—except maybe for Ben, she thought, not altogether surprised. After all, behind the steel of that forceful exterior was a tender side she'd glimpsed on more than one occasion, the various facets of his character fascinating her, drawing her unwilling to him, from that devastating sexual magnetism, his humour, even the darker side of him, his passionate temper, his moods. And then there was that cold, practical side, the man who took ruthless decisions, the side that had made him the governing hand behind a multi-million-pound success story and made the most respected of men respect him, and others, like her, just a little bit intimidated by him, she acknowledged truthfully to herself when they were in the car, leaving the stifling city behind.

'And now it's my turn,' he said when they reached the Halt, taking the crutches Clem handed him to get out of the car.

Apprehension clawed at Sasha's stomach as she realised he was talking about her fresco.

'I warned you I'd never done anything that big before,' she was already worriedly attempting to justify as she followed his chair across the hall, because he hadn't seen it since its early stages. But he merely gestured for her to precede him into the garden room, his expression uncompromisingly detached.

It was, after all, his house, Sasha thought, swallowing, feeling, as he wheeled himself across to the painting, how one of his business associates might feel, waiting for him to make the decision that could make or break.

'Is this really what I asked for?' he exhaled, without taking his eyes off the painting, although his voice was so cool and toneless that she couldn't tell whether he meant it favourably or not. 'Well, it certainly reflects your character. Unsophisticated. Spontaneous. Decidedly adventurous...' He grimaced at her riotous brushwork in the vivid flora, the bold splashes of colour against her sensitive impression of ripe wheat. And suddenly he swung his chair round, his expression a mixture of puzzlement and...what? Censure? she thought, her stomach muscles knotting as he breathed with something not entirely unlike anger, 'Why the devil have you been wasting time——?'

A sound in the doorway cut him short, his mother's, 'I'm sorry, Rex, I didn't realise you were back,' impinging on Sasha's ears. Lorraine was with her, both women looking elegant in their riding gear. But Sheila couldn't have known how untimely her interruption was, Sasha thought, feeling dismayed by Rex's reaction, wondering what he'd been about to say. Didn't he like the result of all the long hours she'd put in? she thought unhappily, somehow managing a wan smile as his mother and cousin came in. 'I told Lorraine she had to see our fresco now it's completely finished.' She smiled appreciatively at Sasha.

'Oh, I see. So it's *our* fresco now, is it?' Rex drawled, transferring his rather quizzical glance from his mother to Sasha.

Unable to meet that grey gaze, she lowered hers. Was that hint of a smile merely for the benefit of the others?

'I suppose it's quite good if you're into frescos,' Lorraine supplied ungenerously, the gold of her tilted head set off by the black riding jacket. 'You're the ones in the long term who have to live with it after all—and Aunt Sheila's obviously smitten. What about you, Rex?' The blue eyes turned his way were almost beseeching him to agree with her, Lorraine, and Sasha held her breath. Would he criticise her in front of the others?

She felt almost queasy as she saw him glance up again at the fresco, saw the strong emotion that marked his face. And her pulse seemed to stop when he caught her in the dark wake of his gaze and, as though there were only the two of them in the room, said softly, 'It's definitely worth losing London Bridge for.'

'What on earth are you talking about, Rex?'

'Only that I was saying when you came in that I don't know why she spends her time painting pretty pictures for calendar companies when she has a talent like this.'

His response to his mother's baffled query barely registered, or the fact that Lorraine was saying nothing. Sasha felt her cutting glance, though, like a tangible thing, realising that the younger woman had obviously noticed that silent communication between her and Rex, but suddenly she didn't care.

He liked it! With a heart-stopping joy, she was unaware of the degree of warmth she communicated to him in her smile, or that her gaze held his a little too long to go unnoticed by the other two. And suddenly, from far away, it seemed, she heard Lorraine's voice, too affected, too light, strung with desperation.

'We're going riding, Rex. Are you coming with us?' Her words pierced the blissful little bubble surrounding Sasha, and invoked Sheila's equally shocked,

'Lorraine!'

'You knew what I meant!' She made a pouting show of penitence as she met Rex's glowering hostility. 'I meant did you want to come and see us off,' she amended quickly, clearly unnerved by that daunting mood she had provoked, yet fooling no one. Jealousy had cut into her like cruel spurs, her obsessive love for Rex impelling her to lash out at him in the only way she knew how. 'I suppose you'll be leaving us— now that the painting's finished.' The smile she flashed at Sasha trembled with wounded resentment. Lorraine was making a fool of herself, Sasha thought, close to pitying her. Pray heaven she never let a man know he'd affected *her* like that!

'I . . . well, I——' she started, embarrassed, not sure what to say. She still hadn't been able to contact her mother to get those receipt numbers for the cheques, and the loan Rex had given her had almost been swallowed up with day-to-day living expenses, fuel for her car and her passport photographs, as well as the passport itself. 'I suppose——'

'Sasha's staying here.' Rex's voice cut decisively across hers and the look he sent her was hard and challenging, defying her to protest. And when she didn't, too embarrassed to raise the issue of her lack of funds in front of the others, he said, 'See?' With his emotions under rigid control, he was smiling at Lorraine now, that lethal smile that could break a woman's heart if she were weak enough, Sasha thought with a little shudder. 'Now go off and enjoy your ride, there's a good girl, and when you get back perhaps we can discuss that extension you mentioned for the salon.'

Which meant that, while Lorraine's parents were pretty well-off, she obviously still turned to Rex for financial backing, Sasha deduced, as the beautician sent her a killing look in contrast to Sheila's good-humoured retreat, and stormed off across the hall.

'For heaven's sake, Rex.' Sasha's hands came to rest on the back of one of the cane chairs, and, feeling he'd been unnecessarily patronising towards his cousin, 'She isn't a child.'

'No?'

Running absent fingers along the smooth cane, Sasha took a deep breath. 'She's in love with you,' she said, her chest tightening when a black eyebrow lifted slightly, querying the tremor in her voice.

'She only thinks she is.'

'She's twenty-two!' If he couldn't see the woman was crazy about him, he had to be blind! she thought, hesitating before saying, 'And very beautiful.'

'Yes.'

So why this deep, gnawing ache to hear him agreeing with her? Because she sensed that the only thing stopping him from marrying her was his inability to walk?

'Where are you going?'

She had turned to leave the room, but his chair was blocking her exit, swivelling round before she could escape.

'Looking around London might be exhilarating but it's also exhausting—I need a bath to revive,' she bluffed, because right then all she wanted was to get away from him.

He wasn't that prepared to let her, however—that dominant will ruling, subjecting her pale, tense features to a probing scrutiny. 'But you'll stay?'

He was telling her rather than asking, and she shrugged. 'Until it's possible for me to leave—yes.'

'And supposing it isn't?' He smiled as though the idea appealed to him. 'You've only another two weeks in this country. Your mother might well be away for as long.'

'That's hardly likely,' Sasha stressed, but even so a small dart of panic shot through her. She was far too wound up over Rex Templeton as it was. And, though he might have a tight rein on his undeniable desire for her, the physical attraction that existed between them was growing daily, and all the more intense for being controlled. The only thing was, what she felt for him was something far more than just physical, she admitted to herself now, so that if she stayed much longer she didn't know how she was ever going to tear herself away.

However, that problem looked like resolving itself far more quickly than she had anticipated when her call to New York was answered the very next day.

CHAPTER SEVEN

'IT'S OK, Mom. Don't worry, I'm fine!' Sasha stressed, despairing of her mother's aptitude for worrying as she came off the phone. 'Moms!' She smiled helplessly at Sheila who had just come into the drawing-room. And, realising, 'Gosh, I'm sorry,' she said, looking sheepish. 'Only you aren't quite like mine!'

'It's a mother's prerogative—to worry,' Sheila sided amiably. 'But no. Rex is too much his own man—far too independent—to let anyone else try to run his life.'

'No,' Sasha agreed wryly. She'd like to see anyone try! 'I just wish I could convince my mother I'm not sixteen any more,' she sighed, and knew that familiar quickening of her blood as she heard the squeak of the wheelchair in the hall.

Without even saying anything to him, he knew. She saw it in the hard narrowing of his eyes before he directed the briefest glance towards his mother, who promptly left.

'Success?'

Sasha nodded. 'Mom's going to the apartment this afternoon for those receipt numbers so I can get those cheques replaced as soon as I pass them on to the bank. They said it might take two or three days. Then I can reimburse you for the loan you kindly made me and then if it's all right with you...' this with a little catch in her voice '...what I mean is...I can't justifiably stay here any longer.' Why did it feel such sheer agony to be saying it?

He wheeled himself in then, that dark countenance crossed with hard, inflexible lines. 'Why not?'

A myriad reckless reasons screamed wildly through her brain. Because you love Lorraine Faraday! And because I—I'm so unbelievably attracted to you...!

She pulled her thoughts up quickly. 'You must agree.' Why had it come out like a plea?

'I don't.' His expression was grim—uncompromising. 'And it isn't *all right with me*.' His knuckles were white as he gripped the wheels of his chair, throwing her own phrase back at her with inexorable mockery. Surely he didn't think her that ungrateful...? 'We'll discuss this tonight—over dinner,' he stated roughly. 'I've got a client to see in Windsor who'll probably keep me tied up all day—but I'll be back by seven—so be ready.'

'But I——'

His determination silenced her, because he had already turned his chair around, and she could only breathe a sigh of relief that at least, it seemed, he would be taking her out to argue the matter with her— which meant that he didn't intend pursuing the discussion in front of Lorraine.

Anyway, he could say what he liked. She'd be booking into a guest house as soon as she had her money, she resolved adamantly—for her own piece of mind, if nothing else! And, careful to avoid Lorraine, she spent most of the day in her room working on her *Corn Dolly*, before deciding it was time to get ready.

Rex hadn't said where he was taking her, so she wasn't entirely sure what she should wear. Not that she had much choice, she thought, grimacing at the lack of anything sophisticated in her wardrobe. He knew she wasn't exactly the last word in designer fashion, so if he hadn't borne that in mind when he'd extended the invitation, then that was his problem, not hers. Nevertheless, she couldn't help being concerned about how ill-equipped she was for the type of upmarket restaurant which Rex would naturally aspire to as she stepped into a full white cotton skirt that moved gently against her calves, and teamed it with a string-laced white bodice.

The look was ultra-feminine, but the straps of the top were cut too close to hide those of her bra, and so she dispensed with the undergarment altogether, hoping that Rex wouldn't notice.

A soft, flowery mist enveloped her as she came down into the hall and she wondered if it was that sultry look to her eyes created by an uncustomary smudge of blue shadow that produced a discreet lift of brows from the waiting Clem.

'Mr Rex says we're to meet him there,' he told her in his usual curt fashion, though he opened the front door for her with all the courtesy imbued in him by two generations of Templeton men. She even fancied he was softening towards her these days.

'Where are we going, Clem? Have you forgotten something?' she asked, leaning forward on her seat when, having left the Halt, the BMW suddenly turned back into the grounds, through another entrance about a quarter of a mile along the road.

He didn't answer, and Sasha gave a little shrug, sitting back. The road, though, didn't lead back towards the house. It sloped away, down through the trees, towards the river. Obviously, she decided, he was taking a short cut to one of the villages.

It was a beautiful evening, pink-hued, with just a touch of breeze, and Sasha closed her eyes, enjoying the warmth of the low sun. She could hear the quiet gurgling of a brook; the sudden, repetitive cooing of a wood-pigeon. And then suddenly the car was pulling up and she opened her eyes, meeting the ivy-clad ruin of what once must have been a summer-house.

She looked bemused at Clem as he came round and opened her door.

'Orders, Sasha,' he said expressionlessly.

'What...?' Puzzled, she grabbed the burgundy silk shawl she'd brought with her and stepped out. Strange, too, that he'd never called her by her first name before. 'Why here, Clem?' she laughed, glancing back at him.

'Have a good evening,' he wished her, getting back into the car, and, to her utter amazement, started the engine and drove away.

She had never been this far down on the estate before and, frowning, Sasha glanced up at the ancient building. It was a controlled ruin—probably listed like the house—and one she remembered seeing in better repair in a painting in the hall.

Now, as her curiosity brought her round to the side of its crumbling exterior, she came to a surprised and devastated halt.

The view was spectacular: a quilt of green and gold where the ripe wheat fields met the emerald of other crops, rising gently on the other side of the river. But it was the sight before the ancient, pillared belvedere that held her spellbound.

A round, wrought-iron table stood on the terrace above the silent river, laid with an intimate feast for two. The sun streaked pink across the damask cloth, striking fire from the silver cloches and the plain silver candelabrum in the centre. And Rex was sitting, arm stretched across the back of one of the crescent-shaped iron seats that curved around the table, smiling lazily up at her.

'You'll forgive me if I . . . don't get up.'

'Goodness!' He was wearing a loose-fitting, long-sleeved white shirt with dark trousers and he looked a knock-out, and she laughed, suddenly nervous. 'When you take someone to dinner—you take them to dinner!'

He gestured to the twin-cushioned seat opposite his own. 'I thought it would appeal to your uncomplicated taste,' he said, pouring champagne.

How well you know me, she thought—even in this short time—realising with some surprise that the seasoned Clem must have gone to a lot of trouble to arrange all this for his employer. But she said only, 'You're a very clever man.' After all, wasn't his sole intention to persuade her to stay?

His smile acknowledged it. 'And you,' he said, lifting his glass to salute her, 'are an incredibly beautiful woman.'

She blushed, grateful for the distraction of a jay that flew, shrieking, across the belvedere, its blue and claret colouring enhanced by a reddening sun.

'Are you hungry?'

She laughed, needing the release of tension, and said, 'What would you do if I said no?'

'Why don't you try me and see?'

I'm not that silly, she thought as his silken challenge sent a delicious little shiver through her.

'Don't worry,' she laughed, 'I'm starving! So much so, I could eat a horse!'

'Sorry—I'm afraid Mother couldn't spare one.' His soft laughter echoed caressingly over hers.

'In that case I'll just have to make do with this.' She pretended a huge sigh of disappointment as he lifted the silver cloches to reveal a starter of marinated artichokes, and a delicious main course of poached salmon and various exotic salads, all of which she tucked into with relish—her appetite sharpened by the fresh air—and, of course, the champagne.

'Don't drink too much,' Rex advised as he filled her glass for the second time.

'Why not?' she giggled, having no intention of doing so. She just liked arguing with him, finding even that a stimulus in itself.

'Because I want you sober.'

Why? she wondered, swallowing. 'Wouldn't it make it easier for you, if I were inebriated, to get me to agree to what you want?'

He merely shrugged, bringing her attention to those solid shoulders, to the feathering of black hair beneath the dark strength of his throat.

'Don't worry.' She gave a tense little laugh. 'I already realise that where differing opinions are concerned I'll need all my wits about me to be able to stand up to you.'

'Now there you have the advantage over me,' he said grimly, a hard cynicism slashing his features as he poured himself more champagne.

Of course. How tactless of her, she thought, hurting for him, and, silently berating herself, glanced away.

The sun was almost setting now, turning the landscape above the winding river crimson with fire. In one of the top fields a harvester still worked, its engine a distant drone, the grain it was cutting sending up a cloud of dust behind it, the subtle freshness of the gathered crop drifting towards them, with the hint of grass-fire, on the air.

'Why do they burn the stubble?' Her eyes were fixed on the smoke rising like purple-grey pillars in the distance, and, wanting to lessen his pain, her voice mischievously low, she said, 'Do they do it in case there are any evil corn spirits lurking about, do you think?'

'Very possibly.' His smile was a flash of ivory—relaxed now—as he spooned the dark chocolate of a Kirsch-laced mousse, sharing her fantasy. 'It could also be a way of keeping infestation down to a minimum—preventing serious pest damage to the following year's crop—as well as guarding against various soil deficiencies.'

'Now you've spoilt it!' she laughed. 'I like pretending.'

'Do you?' His voice was sober as he lit the candles with a lighter he took from his pocket. Clem's, she decided, watching the two bright wicks flare into life, illuminating those hard, disciplined features. 'Then let's pretend you aren't an American and due to go home in two weeks—much less with even more imminent plans to leave my house!'

'Rex, please——' She dropped her spoon into her dish, praying for resistance. He couldn't make her stay there. He couldn't!

'Why are you so determined?'

What could she say? I'm in too deep not to get hurt? How could she? she thought, and with a little shudder reached round for her shawl over the back of the seat, drawing it up around her shoulders.

'Are you cold?' Rex's face .was touched with concern.

'Not really.' How could she add that it was her fear of him—of her feelings for him—and not the temperature that had produced that little shiver?

The breeze, though, had freshened, bringing fragments of chaff pattering across the terrace.

'Oh, look!' It was swirling, as if in a mini-whirlwind, caught helplessly on the current. Fascinated, Sasha watched it lifting higher and higher before the wind suddenly died away, scattering small strands of gold across their table. 'I've never seen anything like it!' she gasped, amazed.

'No.' Rex flashed her one of those crooked, heart-stopping smiles. Then huskily, 'There's something about that that reminds me of you.'

That raw quality to his voice made her look up quickly. Was that how he saw her? she thought. Like straw on the wind? Buffeted by her emotions? Because suddenly she felt as though she was being consumed by his.

Caught by the raw intensity of his gaze, she could almost touch his emotion, feeling hers opening itself to him, unchained and unchallenged, while it dawned upon her then why he'd been so angry with her in the beginning, having to watch her—a healthy young woman—taking chances with her life while he...he didn't even know if he'd ever walk again!

Oh, God, *I love you*!

The realisation shook her like an earth-tremor, and quickly she reached for her glass. But her hand was shaking so much that, clumsily, she knocked it over, sending liquid gold spilling over the cloth.

'Oh, no!' The shawl slipped from her shoulders as she jumped up, dabbing hectically at the damp cloth with her serviette. 'I'm sorry. It's all over your side...'

'Leave it!' Hard fingers grasped her wrist, their touch like a flame to dynamite, shooting off rockets in her blood.

'I can't, I——'

'I said leave it!' His grip tightened as, panicking, she tried to pull away. 'For goodness' sake . . . !' His voice was hoarse, jerky as he shoved hard at the table—pushing it away with the sound of iron scraping stone, his action sending glass teetering, tinkling into fragments against china and steel as he dragged her down across the iron seat, his arms crushing her to him, while his mouth descended, hard and hungrily, over hers.

Instinctively she struggled, resistance her only defence against her hopelessly raging feelings for him. But her need was as desperate as his, and, impassioned, suddenly she was giving in to her physical and emotional demands, clinging to his warm strength as she submitted to his kiss with a wild, reckless hunger she had never known before.

His passion blotted out the dusk, the drip of spilled wine and the trill of crickets in the grass, her senses feeding only on the feel of those lips raining kisses over her face, her throat, her hair, on the sound of his laboured breathing that told her how much he wanted her, and the hard caress of his hands which were suddenly tugging impatiently at the strings of her bodice.

'Oh, *yes*.' His palm against the soft warmth of her breast sent a spasm of raw need through her. His touch, though, was tender, despite the fierce heat of his passion, bringing her arching against him with a small cry of wanting. A wanting she had known ever since that first kiss. No, before that, she thought, if she were truthful . . .

'Sasha.' Against her hair, he breathed her name like an agonised prayer. She felt the shudder go through him as he inhaled her perfume, his breathing harsh and ragged. 'Your skin's like pale silk.'

She sucked in her breath from those cool fingers playing over her midriff, shifting her position slightly to allow them to slip beneath the elasticated waist of her skirt, feeling no betrayal towards Ben now, only an infinite, unbearable longing for those hands—Rex's hands—to possess her utterly, for him to——

'No!' Sitting upright, roughly he pushed her from him. 'It's unfair to me—and it's unfair to you!' Head thrown back, he was staring up at the night sky, jaw clenched tightly as he fought an inner battle for control. 'Forget it ever happened,' he rasped.

'Rex, please . . .' Frustration was a physical ache, and unwittingly she laid her hand on his arm, flinching as he shrugged it away.

'For heaven's sake! Where's your common sense?' he said roughly. 'If you want to get burned, why don't you just go and stick your hand over those candles? It might be more painful physically, but at least— emotionally—you won't get hurt!'

A twinge of the pain he had referred to made itself felt deep inside her and she stared at the flickering flames that were burning more brightly as the night closed in.

'What makes you think I'm emotionally involved?' she said in an unsteady voice, wondering if, in spite of what he had said the previous day, he was warning her off because of Lorraine.

'Conceit.' He gave an imitation of a smile—cynical—self-mocking. 'I also know that commitment's important to a woman like you, otherwise it would have been easy to seduce you that first night in the library—as I sorely wanted to—if loyalty hadn't been such an enduring quality with you. But if you want a brief fling, go out and get it with your go-getting boyfriend, Gavin Chase. I'm sure he can meet all your requirements. At least with him you won't be limited to only half a man—lumbered with a cripple for a lover!'

'You shouldn't say that!'

His hopelessness was tearing into her, along with his allusion to her wanting a brief fling—with anyone. But he was scarred as much emotionally from being rejected before as by his physical wounds, she realised achingly, recoiling from his hard, derisive, 'No? You think I'm a prize catch, do you?' His laugh went through her, bitter and mirthless. 'You think it's a turn-on—being tied to a blasted chair? Then if you think that . . . !' She let out a small cry as roughly he pulled her back across him. 'Stay here! Don't go back to America! Stay here and marry me, you optimistic little fool!'

His kiss was almost savage, his arms practically brutal, hurting her with their impassioned strength—but she didn't care.

He didn't love Lorraine! That was all her screaming brain could grasp, her thoughts swirling with the shock of what he had just said. His mouth on hers, though, was relentless and demanding, those hard hands urgently seeking every inch of her yielding softness.

'Oh, yes, yes!' In a joyous frenzy she let her arm snake up around his neck, thrilling in the feel of that thick black hair between her fingers, her heart wanting to burst in its own song of surrender as he pulled down the straps of her top and, supporting her across his arm, dipped his head to the creamy mound of one breast.

She groaned deep in her throat, closing her eyes against the exquisite pleasure he was creating for her as desire spread outwards from her breasts, a pulsing, feverish heat that had her writhing against him, her body shaken by spasms, unable to have enough of that burning, rousing mouth.

She wanted all he could give her, to give herself in return, and against the heavy thunder of his heart she heard herself sobbing, 'Oh, yes, my love. Yes. I'll marry you! I'll marry you!'

He lifted his head to look down on her dishevelled hair and flushed cheeks, on her perfect breasts, aroused and bathed gold in the candlelight, and his mouth quirked at one side.

'Is that just sex talking—or do you mean it?' he asked in a ragged, incredulous voice.

'Do you?' Suddenly she was afraid his proposal was too impetuous to be believed, especially as she knew he wasn't the impetuous type.

But his lips against her forehead dispelled her worries, causing a whole host of feelings to shudder through her as he said quietly, 'You should know me well enough by now, Sasha, to realise that I don't jest about important issues.'

No, she thought, which made such a speedy and momentous decision on his part seem so out of character—even if it hadn't been the most senti- mental proposal in the world!

Smilingly, she ran her finger along the uncompromising line of his jaw. 'Neither do I,' she whispered, her eyes misted with love for him, but then a little wince escaped her as he caught her wrist in a painful grip, dragging her hand down.

'Do you realise what you'll be taking on?' he demanded, his expression hard from the doubt etching his features.

'Do you?' she parried lightly, smiling up at him, trying to allay his fears. 'I eat horses and believe in corn spirits—and will probably turn up at your company dinners wearing dungarees!' And, suddenly serious, 'Anyway, you're not going to be like that forever, Rex. We can do it between——'

'But supposing I am?' His hold had tightened inexorably, those words which had seemed wrenched from him pulling his face into an unrelenting mask.

Of course. He didn't try to soften the reality of what could well be, she thought achingly, and, swallowing emotion, murmured, 'I'd want you—no matter what. Nothing will change the way I feel about you,' she uttered guilelessly. Nothing mattered but that he wanted—needed her—and that she needed him.

He laughed, his eyes tenderly amused. 'My dear little nature lover, you really know how to make a man feel special, don't you?' He was tracing the line of her cheek with his finger, evoking a quickening excitement in her as he let it linger briefly against her lips. 'Will you try to please me as much in other ways?'

Excitement spiralled as his hand slid expertly along her body so that all she could do was murmur her acquiescence, her own hands seeking and exploring now, unfastening his shirt to meet the hair-feathered warmth of his skin, stroking, teasing, until he groaned and caught her hand, holding it close to his chest.

'Will you object to a short engagement? And to our announcing it immediately?' And when she couldn't answer, too happy to speak, 'Quite simply, I just want to make you mine as soon as I can—and for the world to know it,' he breathed hoarsely, the depth of emotion she felt emanating from him bringing her nuzzling into him, murmuring her agreement against the musky warmth of his chest.

She knew of the difficulties that lay ahead. But there wasn't a thing, she told herself, that they couldn't overcome together. And it wasn't as though she were a naïve youngster, allowing love to blind her to the hard reality of what marriage to a partner who couldn't walk might mean, her train of thought suddenly compelling her to say, 'What will we tell Lorraine?'

She was looking up at him rather worriedly and was unprepared for his hard, 'To hell with Lorraine!' But then, seeing the concern in her heavily fringed eyes, he chuckled softly, pulling her close to him. 'Trust you to be considering someone else's feelings,' he chided softly, 'at a time like this. But don't worry— I've never given her any indication that my affection for her was any more than that of a cousinly one. In fact, I've made it plain on more than one occasion that it wasn't. She'll get over it,' he whispered, smiling down at her. And it was that tender concern in him— so contrastive to that stronger side of him—that made her love him so much, Sasha thought, drawing in a breath from the intensity of her feelings for him when he touched his lips lightly to her temple and murmured, 'Leave it to me. I'll break it to her gently. I promise.'

The following morning Sasha rang her parents before she was even dressed, to tell them about her forthcoming engagement to Rex. And though she expected reservations from them—and particularly her mother—when she told them her husband-to-be was an invalid, she was pleased when they respected her decision—as they always did when her mind was made up about something—and wished her well.

'Just as long as he loves you,' came the rare burst of sentiment from her father, so that she responded happily with, 'Of course,' her face aglow, glad that she was in her room so that there was no danger of anyone walking in and seeing the joy and excitement that seemed almost too much for her to contain this morning.

On reflection, though, she couldn't actually recall Rex saying he loved her—not in those precise words. But even without the way he had held her last night— touched her!—just the mere fact of his wanting to marry her told her how he felt. Also, the suddenness of his unexpected proposal assured her that he was as desperate to keep her with him as she was to stay, and murmuring, 'Thanks, Dad,' she rang off, sitting down then to pour out more of her new-found happiness in a letter to her friend, Juliet.

Arriving downstairs, radiant in a white T-shirt and her lemon dungarees, she stopped, hearing a movement in the library.

'Rex?' She hadn't seen him this morning—not since he had reluctantly let her go to her room after Clem had driven them back last night—and, with her pulses leaping, quickly she moved across the hall, only to come to a sudden and embarrassed halt in the doorway.

'Oh!'

It wasn't Rex, but Lorraine, standing there, looking down into the barren fireplace, and as she swung round, resentment manifesting itself on her face, it was evident to Sasha that she had been crying.

'I'm sorry, Lorraine.' It was all she could think of to say, the futile words having an equally futile effect as Lorraine responded with heart-stabbing bitterness.

'Sorry? What have you got to feel sorry about? You've got what you wanted, haven't you?' Her forced little laugh displayed an attempt at composure that was painful to watch. 'Just between you and me, Sasha—is it our money? Or is it really possible actually to *want* a man who's never likely to be able to walk?'

A butterfly, caught on the inside of the window, fluttered hopelessly against the pane, as beautiful and trapped as Lorraine was in her obsession for her cousin. Sasha couldn't help comparing her with the butterfly, sympathetic yet annoyed—and more by the way the girl had spoken about Rex than the things she had said about her—as she responded tightly, 'Without meaning to sound the least bit callous...' and more softly '...you should know, Lorraine.'

Pain seemed to darken the younger girl's eyes. She looked almost as though she might break down, Sasha thought, relieved for both of them when Pharaoh provided a distraction by leaping up on to the windowsill after the butterfly, her generous efforts to save it as she hurried over to pull the cat away rewarded by its searing claws as it shot out of her grasp across the room.

'All right—so you've won!' She felt Lorraine's jealousy as she stared at the reddening marks on her hand. 'But you don't know Rex the way I do. He's hard and he's ruthless. And if you think you can come in here and steal him from under my nose, then I hope you get a taste of how brutal he can be—and the sooner the better!'

She was practically sobbing as she swept out of the room, almost colliding with her aunt.

'I'm sorry about Lorraine.' Sheila looked contrite as she came into the quiet ambience of the library. 'I'm afraid she's hero-worshipped Rex since she was in her early teens, but of course he's never shown her more than the passing indulgence of an older brother. When he had his accident——' those gentle Scots tones were lowered '—not being able to walk—I think she felt he was suddenly somehow more accessible to her. And with the Press always ready to make mountains out of molehills...' She stepped forward, kissing Sasha lightly on the cheek. 'Anyway, I'm very happy for you, dear,' she said kindly, but with that same thin crease between her eyes that had been there the previous night when Rex had told her of their plans. But Sasha was too happy today to let anything bother her too much, and, smiling her thanks, she went over to open the window, releasing the trapped insect into the morning air.

CHAPTER EIGHT

THE next few days, Sasha felt, couldn't have been happier. She had never felt so complete, so whole, she decided through a delirium of ecstasy—not even with Ben.

It was good, too, to be able to look back on her previous engagement without any of the guilt or the pain that had plagued her before. And it was only Rex, with that calm, masculine logic and understanding, who had helped her to achieve that—helped her put things into perspective, she realised, glancing down at the jewel that sparkled so brilliantly on the third finger of her left hand.

The ring she had chosen was a simple golden sapphire, whose colour, she'd told Rex when they had seen it in the jeweller's window, reminded her of the wheatfields and the mellow summer's evening when he had proposed.

'Only an artist could say that!' he'd laughed when he'd slipped it on her finger in the shop. It hadn't even needed to be altered. It was almost as though it had been waiting—made—with her in mind.

'But it's so expensive!' she had breathed, catching sight of the price on the velvet lining of the little box.

'It's peanuts!' he had laughed again, unintentionally reminding her with that simple remark that to him it was. 'Besides, you're worth it,' he'd added softly, and with such a degree of sensuality in his voice that she'd wished the jeweller would melt away, hardly hearing Rex telling him, 'We'll take it.'

It was the first shop they had looked in too, and there had been a smugness about Rex as he had eased himself from his chair on to his crutches and joined her in the back of the car.

'Now you're mine—and don't forget it!' he had warned excitingly, and, pulling her against him, had kissed her with a hard possessiveness that had taken no account of Clem climbing into the front. Only when she had overcome her shyness—at first too aware of the chauffeur—and given him the response he'd been demanding had he finally released her, while Clem, appearing totally unperturbed, had said over his shoulder,

'May I be the first to congratulate you, sir?'

And madam? she had appended silently, guessing that Clem probably saw her as one of his master's newly acquired chattels, though he had extended a brief nod of courtesy in her direction before turning away with a smiling satisfaction she still wasn't sure she hadn't imagined.

That had been two days ago and now, as she stole lightly down the back stairway—the old route to the servants' quarters—careful to avoid meeting any early arrivals to the party that was to make it official, she still couldn't believe how quickly everything had happened.

'Come in.' Just the sound of that deep voice answering her knock sent a small thrill tingling through her, the sight of Rex sitting there on the bed in an immaculate white shirt and dark evening suit making her go weak at the knees.

'Are you ready?' she murmured unevenly.

'Not quite.' That masculine equanimity seemed oddly shaken by the result of the time and effort she had taken over her appearance, his gaze shifting from the hair she had teased into wild waves and which contrasted so well with the fine white gauze of her top to her shadowed lids and her soft creamy mouth that picked up the rich, deep burgundy of her skirt. And softly he said, 'Come here.'

Her legs felt decidedly wobbly as she moved across to him. Ever since that night by the belvedere they had spent very little time alone together, and now her body pulsed with a reckless excitement as he pulled her down on to the bed.

'You shouldn't be allowed in public looking like this!' he rasped, his mouth coming down on hers and igniting a response in her that had her moving provocatively against him, her legs playing against the lifeless length of his while his arms pinioned her to the duvet with the comparative power of steel.

'Oh, God! I want you!' His mouth was devouring hers, his hands familiarising themselves with the soft, aching contours of her body, sliding up into her hair, tugging her head back to burn a trail of kisses along the smooth, scented line of her throat.

'Rex, we shouldn't . . .' It took all of her will to say it, her voice trembling with desire. 'My hair. My lipstick . . . What will the others say if I turn up looking as if I've arrived——?'

'Fresh from my bed?' His eyelids were heavy with passion, and Sasha drew in a sharp breath as he slipped a hand beneath her top and clasped one soft, swollen breast. 'Then it will just show them how I feel about you, won't it?' he said hoarsely.

She sighed softly, shuddering from the sweet agony of what he was doing to her, and he smiled, watching the twin emotions of need and ecstasy chase simultaneously across her face.

'Particularly your friend, Gavin. Why did you have to invite him?' There was an undertone of possessiveness in his voice that excited her.

'Because he *is* my friend.' She smiled dreamily beneath the sheer torment of his caresses and, willing her eyes to meet his, 'Are you jealous?' she teased, deriving a secret pleasure from the fact that he might be.

He laughed, but didn't deny or confirm it. 'Go and put yourself straight,' he said softly, releasing her, 'before the future groom decides the future bride won't be attending her engagement party after all.'

A little *frisson* went through her as she forced herself over to his bathroom, ruffled by the knowledge that if he'd insisted on keeping her there she'd have been powerless to resist.

Looking back, she couldn't recall ever experiencing such an abandonment of responsibility with Ben—an abandonment that would have had her forsaking her guests if Rex had demanded it. True, she and Ben had had their moments of passion, but she'd always been the one in control, the one who decided how far things should go—according to circumstances, the time, her mood. Which made this total enslavement of her senses by a man so scary, she thought with another, sensual little shudder, finding that no amount of make-up could hide the bright glitter of her eyes, or the fullness of her lips, still burning from the hard demands of his kisses. And if anyone else recognised the signs, then they concealed it well, she thought,

relieved, when they went into the imposing hall to greet
the first few guests who were arriving, although she
sensed a few knowing glances from one or two of the
more astute among them—one of Rex's company di-
rectors, Sheila, and, of course, Gavin—as the party
got under way.

'I see Lorraine Faraday's showing the world she
doesn't care,' he commented quietly to Sasha some
time during the evening, catching Sasha standing momentarily alone by one of Sheila's colourful flower
arrangements, quietly sipping a cocktail. 'Who's the
new boyfriend? Some Scandinavian stud she's had
flown over especially?'

Meaning that Lorraine's escort was as devastatingly blond as Rex was dark—and almost as attractive, Sasha thought, glancing in their direction,
except that the man on Lorraine's arm was just a little
too big to retain those good looks forever, that muscle-
bound physique in no way comparable with Rex's lean
strength.

'I'm just happy she came,' she murmured, looking
down into her glass, because secretly she had to hand
it to Lorraine. If she had got nothing else from Rex,
then she had certainly inherited the Templeton dignity,
because even if she was there under family pressure,
which Sasha very much suspected, she was doing her
utmost—and successfully—to put on a brave face.

'She's not the only one who's good at pretending.'
As Frank Sinatra's smooth tones crooned through the
laughter and conversation going on around the ancient
hall, Gavin's remark bore the tip of a pointed sarcasm.

'What do you mean?' Sasha challenged, frowning
up at him. He looked good with a dark lounge suit

emphasising his fair features—the typical young executive—thrusting, ambitious, and clever.

'Only that I thought you weren't getting involved with anyone. You needed time, you told me—because of something that had happened before.'

And she had never informed him about Ben because she hadn't felt close enough to Gavin to share her innermost feelings with him, not the way she had shared them with Rex—as she wanted to share everything with him, not just her thoughts and her emotions, but her body and soul—her whole life.

'This is different,' she sighed heavily, unable even to begin to explain to Gavin how deeply she felt for her fiancé, starting as Gavin shot back,

'I'll say it is! Honestly, Sasha! I know women find him irresistible, but have you really thought about what you're doing? I mean . . . a lively, fun-loving girl like you——'

'Shouldn't be making such a grave error of judgement.'

The interruption had them both whirling round to see Rex's glacial smile. His face was a dark mask, giving nothing away.

Gavin was dumbstruck, Sasha realised, his silence only emphasising his embarrassment, her own concerned, 'Rex . . .' ignored as he went on, unruffled, comparatively cool.

'Why don't you take a look at my library while you're here, Chase? It offers an insight into business that's second to none. Not that you need any instruction in exploiting the opposition's weak points—but a briefing in diplomacy might well do you some good!'

'Well, of all the...!' Gavin looked deservedly chastened as Rex swivelled abruptly away from them. 'Sarcastic devil, isn't he? I didn't know he was behind me——'

'Then you should be more careful of what you say,' Sasha rebuked quietly, feeling for Rex. 'And yes, Gavin, I have thought about what I'm doing.'

'I'm sorry.' Now he looked thoroughly shame-faced. 'It isn't that I'm not delighted for you, because I am. I'm just still thrown by how quickly you managed to snare the catch of the county——' so thrown, in fact, he'd been virtually speechless when she'd invited him to the party over the phone the other day '—and without any real hint of it beforehand. But congratulations, Sasha. I hope you'll both be very happy. And it will certainly be one in the eye for Rosalind Beckington when she finds out.'

Sasha's hair moved like dark fire as she looked at him, frowning. 'Rosalind...?'

'Ooh-ooh! Sorry.' He grimaced. 'I suppose it's in bad taste mentioning an ex at an engagement party. But I told you about her before. That un-feeling——' He checked himself from voicing his opinion of the other woman. 'His long-time steady who didn't stick around after his accident. She's back in the country by all accounts and she's bound to have mixed feelings when she hears her ex has not only survived without her, but has got himself engaged as well.'

'In fact it couldn't have been a nicer homecoming for her, could it?' Sasha tensed as Lorraine suddenly moved into their orbit. She looked lovely as always, a daringly cut black dress setting off her short blonde hair, her brilliant smile concealing any adverse feelings she might still have been harbouring towards Sasha. 'After the way she treated Rex ...' Lorraine shrugged femininely and sipped delicately at her martini. 'Still, like everything about my cousin, his timing's perfect. I believe she's only been back in Suffolk just over a week.'

Sasha had to work hard to keep her expression bland—indifferent. What was Lorraine intimating? That Rex had deliberately announced this engagement ...?

'Excuse me.' Forcing a smile, she pulled herself away from both of them, ostensibly to mingle with the other guests, fingers curling stiffly around her glass. What if this Rosalind Beckington was back? It didn't necessarily mean that Rex had to know about it. And even if he did, what was she letting herself imagine? That he had asked her to marry him just so that he ...

She put a curb on the ridiculous thoughts that were suddenly running away with her. She was being silly, letting a callous remark by Lorraine, who was still clearly jealous, provoke these insecurities. True, Rex's proposal had been sudden and unexpected, but it was obviously the fact that she had been due to fly home next week that had triggered his decision. He loved her. Of course he did! Even if he hadn't exactly expressed himself in so many words. So what did it matter if his long-standing girlfriend was back in the country? She had probably had to come back at some stage, and it was obviously just coincidence that it had been the week that Rex had proposed.

And if she needed confirmation of that, then it seemed she had it over the next ten days or so, because Rex couldn't have been more attentive towards her if he had tried. Flowers arrived by the dozen if he missed a day without seeing her. Mixed bouquets; orchids; and, on one occasion when he had had to break their lunch date, a single red rose.

'Careful. Flowers have a language,' she teased when he came in that same evening, hoping to prompt him into telling her he loved her—craving to hear him say it. 'How do you know I won't misinterpret what you mean?'

'What that means,' he said concisely, indicating the solitary flower she had placed in a vase on the drawing-room mantelpiece earlier, 'is that you're costing me too much money,' so that she had to avert her eyes to hide her disappointment, seeing only teasing amusement in his. Nor had he explained why he had had to break their lunch date, she realised, and she certainly wasn't going to ask him. It was crazy, she thought. He was her fiancé. And yet over the past few days she'd sensed a broodiness about him, something which, despite his attentiveness, made her feel as remote from him as if they were strangers.

'What's wrong?'

Pretending to rearrange the fern she'd put in the vase with her rose, she stiffened, jolted by his startling perception.

'Nothing,' she lied, without looking at him.

'Then leave that damn fern alone and come and sit down—here.' He had reached across and pulled the green padded pouffe against the wheelchair and, half reluctant, Sasha obeyed. 'Did Ben send you flowers?' he enquired with a curious inflexion in his voice.

'No. Not very often,' she responded, noticing the puzzling intensity that lined those handsome features.

What was he imagining? That his rose had somehow reminded her of her lost fiancé and made her upset?

'Am I rushing things too much?' His fingers in her hair produced a sensual little shudder along her spine. 'Is that what the problem is?' he prompted, that deep voice low, concerned.

Oh, God! What could she say? Just tell me you love me. I want to be reassured. Just to know exactly how you feel about me. But she couldn't say it, closing her eyes to conceal their longing because he was bending towards her and his face—his lips—were too close—and all she could do was shake her head.

'It's because of lunchtime, isn't it?' he said. 'Because I didn't shower you with explanations.' Which was part of it, she thought, catching his sudden undertone of reproach. 'Well, I'm sorry, Sasha . . .' he was moving his chair to one side of the pouffe—behind her—and her pulses leaped as he suddenly pulled her back against him, an arm across her breasts '. . . even husbands and wives don't have to map out every detail of time spent away from each other, so you're just going to have to accept—particularly with a job like mine—that this sort of thing's going to happen from time to time.' And he had no intention of enlarging upon the subject—nor, suddenly, did she want him to, because he was using the best weapon he had to allay her uncertainties—the drugging power of his kiss.

With her back against his knee, she reached an arm up behind his head to seal his mouth desperately to hers, sighing her need as his hand moved across her breasts, feeling him shudder, knowing he was as aroused as she was, hardly mindful of the fact that at any moment Sheila or Clem, or some other member of staff, might come in and surprise them. And perhaps he'd thought of that too, because, bringing his arm up to rest across her shoulders, he said raggedly, his lips in her hair, 'Not now, Sasha. Not here—and not yet. But I'll make love to you—when the time is right—and when I do you won't have any doubt as to where my loyalties lie. Now tell me...' gently he stroked the dark shining hair dishevelled from his kisses '...what did you do instead of meeting me today?'

'I went swimming,' she murmured, still drugged with desire, though not sufficiently to fail to sense the sudden stiffening of his body.

'What—alone?'

'Yes.'

'Not with Gavin?' Those previously gentle fingers twisted painfully in her hair, dragging her head back across his knee.

'*Rex*...' She groaned, looking up into the dark rigidity of his features, hers contorting with discomfort, and she sat up as he suddenly freed her, her expression pained. 'Of course I didn't go with Gavin.' How could he even think that? 'I'm engaged to you.'

'That didn't seem to stop you playing badminton with him the other day.'

'That was different!'

'Was it?'

'Yes, I told you.' She turned to face the scepticism in the slaty quality of his eyes. 'He was playing a doubles match with his sister and she wasn't well, and so as not to let the others down at the last minute he asked me.'

'And like the ever-helpful little thing you are you went along?'

'Yes. Wouldn't you?' she challenged, hurt by his unreasonable attitude, only realising, when she saw the hard cynicism on his lips, what she had said. 'I'm sorry. I meant ... Oh, you know what I meant!'

'Forget it,' he rasped, a bleakness in his eyes quickly veiled before he swung his chair round, leaving her with only the sight of those powerful shoulders as he wheeled himself away.

The next morning he was gone before she was even up, and she was glad, therefore, that they had at least managed to patch things up eventually the night before. Rex had apologised, too, for being away so much, even offering her some suggestions for the final illustrations she was doing for her *Corn Dolly*, his appreciation of the work she had put into the little book with their subsequent discussion and his interest in her future helping to put things back on an even keel. Finally, pulling her down beside him on the library sofa, he'd kissed her long and hard before he'd let her go to bed, so that this morning she was nursing a warm contentment when Sheila met her on the stairs and asked if she would take a call from Dee on Rex's private line.

'He's in conference,' Dee explained when Sasha picked up the phone in his office. 'He said he left before the post and I know he's expecting an important letter with a cheque that just possibly might have been sent to the Halt instead of here. Would you mind opening what there is and letting me know?'

'Even the ones marked "Private and Confidential"?' Sasha laughed after doing—though vainly—what Dee had suggested, because there were a couple of those. One from the Tax Office, she could tell without even opening it, the other handwritten in long, sloping scrawl.

'Secretary's privilege,' Dee chuckled, as Sasha picked up the gold letter-opener again.

But not a fiancée's, she thought, shaken as she scanned the contents of the hand-scrawled letter.

It was an exceedingly personal note, pleading with Rex to respond to telephone messages that had obviously gone unanswered, begging for contact—for the smallest acknowledgement from him—and it was signed simply 'Rosalind'.

'That's all there is.' Sasha dragged herself out of her stunned silence, unable to communicate to Dee that Rex's old girlfriend was writing to him. Not that he'd want Dee to know anyway, she thought, certain of it, and, feeling like an eavesdropper, wondered how he'd react to *her* opening it instead. Perhaps Dee wouldn't have opened anything handwritten, she thought with the guilty knowledge that she should have considered that herself. But surely Rex wouldn't mind if he didn't care anything for the woman any more. But if he did . . .

As Dee rang off, an agony of doubt began to surface in her mind. Supposing this was what he had been hoping for? Supposing Lorraine had been right—that he'd known his old love was back and had announced his engagement deliberately to get even with her?

My goodness! You're paranoid! she told herself. She had to pull herself together. Rex loved her! Otherwise why would he have asked her to marry him? Intelligent people didn't make commitments without being fully committed to that person, as the very word suggested. And Rex was about the most intelligent man she had ever met.

Nevertheless, she didn't want to let him know what she had found in his morning's mail, and, folding the letter back into its envelope, she realised rather desperately that there was no way to reseal it without him knowing that it had been opened. She had slit the envelope right across the top, so it was hardly a question of sticking it back down. She even thought about typing a fresh envelope and sending it back to him through the post. But that would look odd, she thought, as the letter itself was handwritten, and besides, she didn't want to do anything so underhanded, realising that the most sensible thing would be to confront him openly about it. Somehow, though, she couldn't do that, and eventually she decided simply to leave it on his desk and let him mention it to *her* first, as he would be bound to when he saw that it had been opened.

Consequently, when he came out on to the front terrace that evening where she was sitting, painting, she felt her stomach muscles tighten, knowing he had just finished going through the day's post.

'It's lovely.' He was looking down at the pad resting on her knees and the little watercolour figure of her corn dolly with the bright red bow in her hair. 'It'll capture the hearts of all the kids from here to the South Pole.'

The way you've captured mine? she thought, enthralled, as always, by the sheer magnetism of him as he studied her work, her gaze touching on the dark feathering of his lowered lashes, the rich warmth of his skin beneath the mellow sunshine, that lazy, abstracted smile.

'Do you think it'll make me a fortune?' she giggled, but with that same disquieting feeling inside, waiting for him to say something about that letter. But he didn't.

And that could mean that he hadn't read it yet, she thought, although she doubted it immensely, trying to hide her unease behind her smile as he took her hand and bestowed a rather absent kiss upon it, saying, 'If it doesn't, they'll have me to answer to.' And casually, 'You'll have to excuse me, darling, but I've got quite a few phone calls to make inside. Enjoy your painting—and the rest of this lovely evening.' He looked unusually complacent—relaxed—as he viewed the tired roses beyond the terrace. 'I'm going in to get started. I'll see you at dinner.'

So that was that, Sasha thought, putting down her brush, finding her inspiration deserting her with his departure. He couldn't have missed that letter. She had put it near the top of the rest of his mail in the middle of his desk! So maybe he was just waiting for a more opportune moment to bring it up. Still, if he was, it certainly wasn't at dinner, she found herself reflecting later, because Sheila had joined them for the meal, seeking his advice and comments on a racehorse she was thinking of investing in, while Rex had sat there, oblivious to the tension in her, Sasha, looking devastatingly composed. Then afterwards some important customer had kept him on the phone for nearly an hour, after which her mother had telephoned—as she did occasionally to assure herself that her daughter was well and happy—and then, with Rex buried in paperwork following his phone call, they hadn't had an opportunity to relax together again.

She was up early the next morning, determined to see him before he left as he had told her he'd be in the London office for most of the week.

The truth was, she hadn't slept that well and decided to go for a jog through the grounds as soon as
it was light. She was, therefore, tracksuited and
flushed when she joined Rex for breakfast in the
dining-room, the dark stains on her shoes indicating
an early autumnal dampness in the woods.

'You're the most . . . vibrant, spirited creature I've
ever met,' he drawled, putting down his newspaper
and catching her arm to pull her towards him as she
sat down, planting a light kiss on her lips. 'No, keep
it on. You'll cool down at a hell of a rate,' he advised
when she went to remove her top, and so she complied. After all, he knew. Hadn't he told her that he
used to jog regularly every evening through the
grounds to unwind before he had had his accident?
That crease between his eyes, though, seemed to
counter his apparent pleasure in seeing her. As though
he had something on his mind. That letter? she wondered, swallowing.

'Did you catch the post this morning?' she ventured tentatively, trying to appear nonchalant as she
poured herself some orange juice from the glass jug.

'Yes. Thanks,' he added almost distractedly so that
she glanced at him quickly, but he wasn't even looking
at her; he was scanning a paragraph of the folded
newspaper instead, calmly buttering his toast.

'I should start thinking about a trip home,' she said
unsteadily, after taking a long, thirsty draught of her
juice. She didn't want to talk about this. She wanted
to ask him about that letter. Surely he must have read
it by now? And if he had, why hadn't he said something, knowing that she had opened it—seen it? she
puzzled woundedly.

'Do you have to go?'

She had his full attention now and for some reason it was oddly disconcerting. 'I have to—some time.' She gave him a fleeting smile, wondering if it had been genuine regret she'd detected in his voice. 'I'm running out of painting materials and it seems rather ludicrous buying new when I've left so much back home. Also, Mum and Dad are keen to know all about you...' She couldn't look at him as she said it. 'Not to mention my friend, Juliet. There's also the question of an apartment lying idle when it can be benefiting some other needy soul or couple who might be looking for a reasonably priced home. Apart from which...' she pulled a wry face '...I could do with the cash assets myself. I'm going to have to put it on the market soon if... if you're intending I should live on this side of the Atlantic after we're married,' she said lightly, though a little uncertainly, because although he'd talked a lot about the wedding at first he hadn't mentioned it for days. 'I can't leave it all to Mum or Dad to sort out—it wouldn't be fair.'

'No,' he breathed, making her wonder why he sounded less than happy to be discussing it, 'and I do agree that a bride obviously needs funds. But don't be too hasty in getting rid of it just yet—it isn't a good time to sell. Your country's in recession—property prices are at rock-bottom. It would be more to your advantage to leave it for a while—think about selling when the market recovers.'

He was right, of course, she thought, watching him bite into the cool, crisp toast. So why did she feel that he had some other reason for offering that advice beyond his sound professional expertise? Was he having second thoughts about asking her to marry him—second thoughts that had only been strengthened because of that letter?

'I've got a mortgage,' she reminded him, 'which means that my money will still be tied up. And here or in America my financier's still going to want his cheque.'

'Then we'll pay it off,' he said.

Which meant *he* would, Sasha thought, starting to protest as he wiped his hands on a napkin, but then he was moving his chair, close enough to place a silencing finger on her lips.

'I insist,' he said firmly, while her senses were suddenly being fogged by the subtle tang of the aftershave lotion that still clung to the cool, lean hand. 'I won't have you worrying about money. It'll detract from your creative flow. And you've got too rare a talent to waste your energies concentrating on anything else. By the way,' he remembered, catching her hand and brushing her fingertips lightly with his lips, 'I shan't be able to leave as early as I'd planned this afternoon, so we're going to to have to take a raincheck on that afternoon tea. However, if you're still planning to come up to the city today, come and meet me some time after six. I'll be through by then and I'll make it up to you by taking you out to dinner.'

With still no reference to that letter, Sasha realised, watching him leave, telling herself that it didn't matter. But it did. He knew she had seen it—that she'd be dying to know what he intended to do about it. After all, she had a right to know! So why, if the other woman didn't mean anything to him any more, was he refusing to discuss it openly with her? she wondered unhappily.

Telling herself she was getting paranoid again, she pushed it to the back of her mind and got on with her day, spending the morning getting her manuscript and illustrations ready for her publisher. She didn't feel like driving up to town, but, having accepted Rex's invitation earlier, she decided she might just as well stick to her original plan and look for a winter jacket as well. Besides, she thought, a trek around the shops might do her some good, help her get things back into perspective. But she was in no mood for shopping, and she arrived at Rex's office a little earlier than arranged, although it was still late enough for the usual receptionist to have left, and the night-security man was already on duty.

With a friendly word to him, she crossed the plush foyer to the lift, taking it up to the top floor.

The outer office was deserted. Dee had already gone home. But the door to Rex's office was ajar and as she crossed over to it she heard voices coming from inside.

'You're making a mistake.'

'It won't be the first time.' It was Rex, responding to the unfamiliar voice of a woman.

'Not you. At least never one this big. Oh, Rex, can't you see . . . we were right together?'

'Then why did you leave?' The way he said it—with such raw anguish—made the blood turn cold in Sasha's veins.

'I—I was frightened. I couldn't come to terms with it.'

'And now you think you can?'

'Oh, Rex . . .' The woman's voice was low, cracking with emotion. 'You're so hard and cynical now. All right, I was wrong. But please...please don't treat me like this.'

'What do you want to hear me say, darling? That I didn't stop thinking about you? That never seeing you again was more crippling than the knowledge of never being able to walk? How right you were?' His laugh—his words—seemed torn from his lungs, as painfully as the breath Sasha had to drag through hers. She couldn't believe it! His very torment implied he was still in love with the woman even if that wounded masculine pride was keeping him from actually spelling it out!

Listening was a devastating agony as she heard that feminine voice utter almost triumphantly, 'Oh, Rex...'

She wanted to clamp her hands over her ears—tear herself away—but she couldn't move, hearing light footsteps trip across the room, the creak of the wheelchair followed by a small, feminine groan and then silence—the implicating silence of lovers locked in an embrace.

Oh, *no*! Too late, Sasha's hands went to her ears as she battled to stifle her cry of despair. She felt numb, sick, dragging herself from the torturing reality behind that door, back out to the waiting lift.

The security guard waved as she passed, but she wasn't even aware that she acknowledged him as she arrived, half dazed and hurting, in the street.

How could he? she agonised, taking deep breaths to stop the emotional pain from overwhelming her. He'd been putting up a battle in there—with himself— and he'd clearly lost! Rush-hour traffic roared along the road, yet she hardly seemed to notice, her mind on only one thought: Rex still loved Rosalind Beckington.

Making her way back to the multi-storey car park where she'd left the Mini, her first instinct was to go home. But home, she realised, with a sudden dawning irony, was three thousand miles away. And yet she couldn't go back to the Halt—not yet. Not while she was still hurting so much inside.

After paying the parking fee, she drove out of the building, her mind cluttered with harrowing thoughts as she negotiated the busy streets. No wonder he hadn't mentioned that letter! Hadn't wanted to talk about the wedding! It all made sense now if, deep down inside, he'd been struggling against his feelings for Rosalind. And his suggestion this morning that she, Sasha, didn't sell her apartment; that he would clear the mortgage—what was that? Some sort of security? A way of safeguarding her interests and his own by ensuring she wasn't completely homeless, therefore making it easier on his conscience if he decided he couldn't go through with marrying her after all?

She was crying now, her tears hampering her driving, but half angrily she brushed them away. She wasn't sure for how long or how far she drove, only stopping when she reached the coast where she parked her car, walking down on to the dusk-enveloped beach.

A wind was whipping up and the night sky coming in from the sea looked strangely ominous, but she didn't care, kicking out at the sand as she walked, her thoughts as turbulent as the waves washing hard on to the shore.

What was there for them now after what she'd heard back there in Rex's office? Was it over between them? Would he be going back to Rosalind? In that case, how did she herself figure? As just a brief, enjoyable interlude in his life?

Dear heaven, she couldn't think about that!

Hearing the rumble of thunder in the distance, she started back to the car, but she had been walking for longer than she realised and, already dark, it was also raining heavily by the time she reached the Mini. Consequently, in the light, cotton two-piece she had worn with the intention of going out to dinner, she was soaked and shivering when she eventually arrived back at the Halt.

It was late—much later than she'd realised, she thought with a grimace at the hall clock before creeping quietly upstairs, dreading facing Rex, wondering what she'd say to him—what he'd say to her—when she eventually did.

Glad to have made it to her room without anyone hearing her, with her teeth chattering she peeled off her wet clothes and gave herself a vigorous rub down with a towel. Then, warm in a full-length white towelling robe, she was just drying her hair when the door suddenly burst open, drowning her startled cry as it crashed back against resisting steel.

'Where the hell have you been?' Shakily Sasha switched off the hairdrier, shocked not only to see Rex there—in her room—but also by the anger darkening his face, making the veins stand out in his throat above the open-necked shirt. 'Don't you think we haven't all been frantic with worry? What am I supposed to think when I leave my fiancée at breakfast, thinking I'm seeing her for dinner, and no one knows where the hell she is when she hasn't turned up or come back by nearly midnight? We had a date—remember? Or aren't I even allowed the courtesy of a phone call when you decide you want to break it? When something's so important to keep you out this late—alone.'

There was sarcasm in that last word. But how could he accuse *her* of being with anyone else after what she'd heard behind his office door? she thought bitterly.

'I'm sorry.' She shrugged, and laid the hairdrier down on the dressing-table, absently aware now that he had obviously got up here by means of the lift that had only been completed the day before. 'It must have slipped my mind. I didn't realise we'd made any definite arrangements.' And now she was lying. Taking the coward's way out, she thought, too weak—too hurt—to confront him with the truth of what she had heard.

'Oh, didn't you?' He didn't believe her. His eyes alone told her that. They were like slits of daggered slate, penetrating, piercing right through her. 'So what have you been doing all this time? Swimming?' With that barbed cynicism those eyes touched on her damp hair. 'You haven't been in long enough to take a shower—and I was under the impression the public baths closed hours ago. So what *have* you been doing? Running barefoot in the rain with that fawning opportunist, Chase?'

'How dare you?' Sasha's eyes blazed. She wanted to scream at him about all she had witnessed between him and the other woman earlier, but the words seemed to stick in her throat. 'And what if I were? At least he doesn't want me just to ease his own frustrations!' she was hurling back instead, wanting to hurt him as much as she had been hurt, hearing that heartfelt declaration he had made to Rosalind

Beckington, and realised, when she saw the dark emotion graven on his face, that she had overstepped the mark.

His face pale with fury, he wheeled himself in, the bang of the door he threw closed behind him making Sasha visibly wince. She saw those masculine knuckles whitening as he gripped the arms of his chair, his eyes holding anger, but much, much more—a chilling, menacing intent.

She stared at him as all the power in his body seemed to manifest itself in those hands, and with all the combined strength of his will he pushed himself up, out of the chair, to advance with clumsy yet startling purpose towards her.

CHAPTER NINE

'REX ...!' Dazed with shock, Sasha took a step back, her hand going to her mouth as she came up against the bedpost, aware only of those blazing eyes as he lunged, reaching for her before she could move out of his way.

'What's wrong? Don't you prefer me like this?' he laughed harshly at her small, startled cry and, over-balanced by her struggles, brought her crashing down with him on to the bed. 'Isn't that what you want? A man who can walk?'

'No! I mean ...! Oh, Rex, no! Please!' His anger was unremitting and she struggled in vain, fighting both him and the waves of sensation that were coursing through her beneath his weight.

'What are you so afraid of? Don't you like me this way? Or does it destroy your illusion of the pitiable cripple you've got yourself engaged to?'

'Don't!' She was crying, sobbing against his anger, against every one of the cruel surprises to which he had subjected her today; fighting him, but uselessly because he had her wrists pinned at shoulder level, his grip hard and relentless on her soft flesh. 'Rex ...'

She looked up at him and surprisingly, for a few moments, saw the devastating emotion on his face. An emotion that drew a small gasp from her as she recognised pain as deep as her own. Then it had gone, leaving his face a mask of stone, and she made a strangled sound in her throat as his mouth clamped mercilessly over hers.

She struggled to resist, fighting his kiss, his restraining hands and the weight of his hard body that was slowly and insidiously turning her on. But then suddenly he groaned—a sound from deep in his lungs—and at the same time her resistance snapped, like an explosion of wanting way, way down inside her.

Anger turned to passion in a fire of mutual need, her breathing as ragged as his as he suddenly released her hands so that his could map the unresisting contours of her body. Her robe was being ripped open, while with a shared urgency she was tugging at his shirt, revelling in the scent, the feel of that solid masculine body, giving a shuddering gasp from the heat of his hands on her own aching, sensitised flesh.

Oh, God! What was she doing? He was in love with another woman—and she didn't care! She wanted him now! To make him want her! Want her enough to make him love her...

And either instinctively or from experience he knew. He wasn't even fully undressed, but neither was she, lying there in a tangle of dishevelled clothes that neither could care about discarding, their desire too strong to be prolonged. And then she was lost, her troubles submerged beneath a volcano of deafening, blinding sensation, a world where there was only one man and one woman and an unequalled, sobbing joy which suddenly exploded for them both in an eruption of hard, shattering spasms of pleasure.

When she awoke, she was lying in a pool of perspiration. Her whole body ached and she felt clammy and a little bit sick, while at the same time she felt as though she was burning up.

She groaned into the darkness and as though from an agonised dream remembered the angry scene with Rex, the joy as he'd made love to her. But Rex had *walked*! So she must have been hallucinating. Which meant that his lovemaking had been part of the same dream because he wasn't here now, and he could never have left her, surely, without her waking?

She must have lapsed into sleep after that because night seemed fused with day. She heard voices and tried to answer, but they didn't seem to understand what she was saying.

She called to Rex, and thought that at least *he* responded. But how could he, she thought, when Rex loved someone else, and the man who sat beside her on the bed, gently palming her forehead, whispered tender, coaxing words as though he loved *her*?

When she woke again, the fever had broken. She no longer ached and, clear-headed now, she blinked at the mellow sunshine of a September morning.

Desperate for a bath, she slid weakly out of bed—and, realising how unsteady she was, grabbed one of the bedposts just as Sheila Templeton came in.

'You're up!' The woman hurried anxiously across to Sasha. 'Are you sure you're well enough yet? You've been delirious for two days. I can't tell you how worried we've all been—especially Rex. Fancy going off like that in the rain and catching a chill!'

'Is that what it was?' Sasha grimaced, not needing to be reminded of her anguished drive to the coast, of that ugly scene with Rex, and her own bitter words that had spurred him into getting up—walking! But Sheila had said he'd been worried. With a little shiver of sensation she remembered the vehemence of their lovemaking. Had it changed the way he felt about her? she wondered achingly, with a puzzling glance down at the nightdress she couldn't recall putting on.

'You were still in your dressing-gown, half under the duvet, when I came in and decided to send for the doctor,' Sheila commented, aware, her amazed, 'You *must* have been feeling bad to fall asleep like that,' causing Sasha to turn her head to hide her flaming cheeks, as Rex's mother went on, 'I thought you'd be more comfortable in one of your nightdresses.'

'Thanks.'

The last thing she had wanted was to put anyone to any trouble, and she was about to say so when Sheila asked, 'Are you hungry, Sasha? Shall I arrange some breakfast for you?'

She was, but the fever had dehydrated her and her tongue felt like sandpaper, and she said, 'Thanks, but first do you think I could have some orange juice, please?'

'Of course, dear. I'll have it sent up.'

With no mention of Rex walking, Sasha realised, as the woman insisted on running her bath for her, although she knew, without a shadow of doubt, that it hadn't been a dream. So could that also mean that those tender words she had heard him whisper when she was lying there so unwell had been real, too? she pondered wistfully. And found no comfort in remembering that Sheila had said she'd been delirious, so that that, at least, had probably been in her mind, she thought—imagery induced by the very core of her longing.

When she came downstairs, having breakfasted on a lightly boiled egg and toast, and consumed what had seemed like a gallon of juice, she came across Rex in the library.

Sitting there at the table, poring over a book, he didn't hear her come in, the sight of that bowed dark head and those long, skilled hands as he turned a page causing a deep, dull ache in her stomach. Then he looked up with a surprised, 'Sasha!' his strong face lit with a smile as he swung his chair back—away from the table.

'You—you walked,' she reminded him, baffled, her eyes questioning as he seemed, as always, a prisoner of that chair.

'Yes.' He reached across and grabbed a stick that was resting against one of the easy-chairs, and a lump came to Sasha's throat as he brought himself to his striking height, standing there towering over her. 'How do you feel?'

'Wobbly,' she admitted shyly, wondering how he could be so concerned about her when something so wonderful had happened to him. She had to restrain the urge to run to him, bury her face in that softly casual shirt.

'Join the club,' he said with a slanted smile, moving towards her, leaning heavily on his stick.

'How long . . . had you known?' Incredulously, she watched him walking. He was unsteady, it was true, but all it was going to take now was practice, she was sure of that.

'I didn't.' He stopped just a couple of feet away, beside the lithe, graceful figure of the muse. 'I've been trying for months—without success. I couldn't manage to put one foot in front of the other without keeling over. Not until something made me angry enough to——'

Something. Meaning her, Sasha thought as their eyes met, feeling the deluge of colour that washed up over her skin. Walking wasn't the only thing he had mastered in her room the other night. But, eager to keep the conversation from leading in that direction, she enquired, 'Did you tell your mother? I thought she would have said something to me if you had, but she didn't.'

'No.' He slipped his free hand into his trouser pocket. 'I don't mean no, I haven't told her. I mean I asked her not to mention it to you. We had a pretty ugly scene the other night and I couldn't help feeling that I'd helped contribute to your being ill. I didn't want you reminded of that unnecessarily—getting upset. The doctor said you caught a severe chill—I think there was more to it than that.'

She looked at him questioningly, her fingers running idly over the doorknob. His expression, though, was unreadable as he made a contemplative study of her pallid features and darkly ringed eyes, and her evident loss of weight beneath her checked shirt and jeans, and quietly he said, 'Come here.'

His soft command made her pulses throb. Complying, she gasped as one arm caught her to him, so close that she could feel the hard angle of his hip pressing into hers, the firm, solid muscle of his thigh.

'Where the devil did you go to get so cold and wet? You could have contracted pneumonia. Where were you?' It was a soft yet insistent demand.

'I was walking,' she confessed, responding to that authoritative note in his voice. She felt so feeble, she was clinging to his strength, wondering how, when he needed a stick to support himself, he still managed to seem like six feet of invincible rock.

'With Gavin?'

That was what she had led him to believe the other night, but she couldn't lie to him now, her hair softly brushing her shoulders as she shook her head. 'No.'

A fine line drew his brows together as those slaty eyes seemed to bore down into her soul. And then suddenly his lips were brushing against hers, their touch light and undemanding, very gentle.

His scent, his warmth, his strength seemed to invigorate her feeble limbs and her arms slid round him, the soft murmur that escaped her a plea to him to deepen the kiss.

Gently his tongue probed the soft cavern of her mouth, the intimacy sending a flood of desire coursing through Sasha's veins. She felt her breasts blossom and ache, felt the shudder that ran through Rex, and the unmistakable hardening of his body.

His stick clattered noisily against the table-leg as both his arms came round her now, and cautiously he staggered back against the table with her, using the corner for support, his mouth fused to hers as he virtually lifted her against the hard, pulsing length of his masculinity.

'You bewitch me—I swear it.' He sounded almost angry, his breath dragging laboriously through his lungs. But, whether he minded or not, his mouth still demanded from hers, the heat of his hands through her shirt evoking memories of their hard warmth on her body the other night until she was like a rag doll in his arms, weak beyond the after-effects of her chill.

'Rex . . .' It came out as a breathless sigh. Because surely, whatever else she had imagined, his actions now showed that he loved *her*—not Rosalind Beckington?

Suddenly, though, he was summoning enough control to draw back, to utter, 'You're not well enough for this,' and with a light tap on her backside set her gently back down on her heels. 'Besides,' he said with a wry pull of his lips, 'if we keep doing this without any forethought, it could result in other consequences. You could get pregnant—and you wouldn't want that, would you?'

Wouldn't she? She shook her head, lowering clouded eyes. Why did he sound so sure about what she would want? And how did he know she wasn't pregnant already? Or was he avoiding mentioning the possibility of that because it conflicted with his own wishes? She was too unsure of him—even though she was wearing his ring—to ask.

He was looking around for his stick, and Sasha stooped to retrieve it.

'Thanks,' he said, taking it from her, catching her hand with his free one as she made to withdraw. 'Why did you want me to think you were with Gavin?' he asked sombrely, and his expression was sombre too, the fine lines at the corners of his eyes and mouth appearing deeper than usual, as though he was tired from overworking or something.

Because I heard you with Rosalind—in your office! She wanted to unburden herself of this torturing knowledge and say it. But she couldn't—even now— too afraid of what his answer might be, and so she shrugged, murmuring, 'I don't know.'

His touch was stirring that familiar ache in her again, and she glanced down at that broad thumb absently stroking her wrist where the blue vein pulsed. But then he nodded, almost indiscernibly, his mouth compressing as though her answer had satisfied him

in some way. And then he kissed her, but un-
affectedly, on the forehead, which didn't seem to tally
with the tremor in his voice, she thought, when he
said, 'Take it easy today and if you're a very good
girl I might let you go outside tomorrow.' And with
a wry smile wiping any lurking emotion from his face,
'Now go and put your feet up before I have to carry
you back to bed myself!'

It was in fact two days before Sasha felt strong enough
to take a walk, and the sun was so pleasantly warm
that she stayed outside for a while, occupying the seat
in the shrubbery where she had had that first conversation with Dee.

'You look so... relaxed—it seems a pity to disturb
you.'

So absorbed had she been in the magazine she was
reading that Rex's approach made her jump.

'I'm sorry.' He was smiling contritely as he came
to sit down on her left-hand side, stick resting idly
between his legs. He was walking a little—albeit with
difficulty—each day, but it was still hard to believe
that he'd made it almost from the garden room, his
chair abandoned outside on the flags.

'I'll have to put you on a leash if you get too adventurous!' she jested.

'Like a dog and faithful servant?' A smile touched
his lips, but he knew as well as she did that he had
the controlling hand—where her emotions were concerned, if nothing else.

'Somehow I can't see you in that role!' She laughed
lightly and swayed unconsciously towards him. She
wanted him to kiss her, put his arm around her, but
he did neither. He was watching the antics of a wren

that kept disappearing among the stones of an ancient rockery beyond the mossed statue of the fountain.

'Oh, I'm already enchained, Sasha—if not in the literal sense. You're surely not naïve enough not to realise that. I don't mean this in a detrimental way— but you weren't a virgin. You knew how out of control I was the other night. As far as chemistry goes, no other woman ever had the power to make me want her so much at first glance the way you did—sitting there like a helpless, injured, irresponsible child I wanted both to protect and to take to bed. Your biggest mistake was letting me know that it was mutual—although I suppose no man can help being attracted to that natural sensuality of yours. It's sexier than all the artificial aids that most women use to attract men put together. In fact it's lethal. And the amazing thing is you're not even aware of it, are you?'

His voice was almost remonstrative and she slanted a glance up at him. 'I'm sorry,' she apologised woundedly. Why was he talking to her like this? And using the past tense as though... She clamped the thought rigid before it could take shape. 'I can't help being myself.'

'Exactly,' he breathed. 'It's that innocence that makes it so darn lethal. Heaven help a man if you were really trying! I don't think he could have you and still stay sane. But sex can be a pretty dominant emotion...'

She wasn't sure what he was getting at; couldn't think either because he was leaning towards her with his arm across the back of the seat, and she became conscious of the dark intensity in his eyes before his head suddenly dipped, obscuring her vision.

His lips moved lightly yet sensually on hers, but when she swayed towards him with a small murmur he suddenly drew back.

'It takes more than this to make a marriage,' he said quietly.

She looked at him quickly, wondering what he was trying to say, claws of ice seeming to clutch her heart as she glanced down at the smaller hand resting in his, saw that broad thumb circling over her ring.

'The other night I——' He broke off, seeming to find difficulty choosing the right words. 'You were right. I *have* been totally selfish. OK, so I'm on my feet—after a fashion. But no one can guarantee any more miracles—that things will ever be quite as they were before the accident.' He looked at her then, his expression bleak and empty. 'What I'm trying to say is ... I won't hold you to the engagement.'

She had known it was coming. Known, even though her mind had rebelled against accepting the truth. Even so, that didn't help to lessen the blow of hearing him actually saying it.

Colour draining from her face, she uttered, 'You mean ... you're breaking it off?'

She wondered if her voice betrayed the despair she could feel seeping through her as he responded flatly, 'No, I'll leave that entirely to you.'

Why? she wanted to scream, her tortured eyes alone asking the question, because she knew why. She might have believed his talk about being selfish—that he was doing it for her—offering her a way out. But after that scenario she'd witnessed between him and Rosalind the other night there wasn't any doubt in Sasha's mind that he still loved the woman. And now that he wasn't totally confined to a chair ...

She had to hold her breath against the weight of tears that seemed to be pressing down on her. He was leaving it to her, he'd said, because even now, she thought, in spite of his loving someone else, that dignity and honour of his wouldn't let him simply renege on a promise?

'Well, that's that, then, isn't it?' She could feel her lips trembling and yet it was amazing how she could still manage to smile.

A light breeze was ruffling his hair, hair her fingers ached to touch and knew they would never be able to again as he frowned and said, 'That's all you have to say?'

Of course. He didn't know she'd overheard him with the other woman. But what did he expect her to say? I love you. Please don't do this to me! She had her dignity, too. Why couldn't he leave it like that?

'What else is there to say, Rex? We both made a hasty decision. Let's not make it harder on each other by prolonging the agony...' Grabbing her magazine, she jumped up, unable to sit there and discuss the end of their engagement as calmly as though they were talking about the weather. She had to get away.

'Hold on!' He caught her arm, stopping her in mid-flight, holding her there in front of him like a desperate, trapped animal. 'You can't just walk away from it—pretend it hasn't happened. There's one thing at least to take into consideration. The fact that you might be pregnant.'

She couldn't look at him as she uttered, 'Unlikely,' not trusting herself not to break down from the torturous reminder of their lovemaking.

'But you're not on the Pill. You said so yourself—so you don't know for sure.'

Her eyes still averted, she shrugged, not realising how careless she'd appeared until he practically shook her.

'For goodness' sake! Don't you care enough even to want to provide our child with a future?'

His fingers bit into her arm and with a wounded anger she shook them off. How could he talk about caring when he was the one who wanted to terminate their relationship? When he was the one who was in love with someone else?

'For a start it's purely hypothetical,' she returned, keeping her chin high, the only way she could face him without giving in to tears. 'And if it isn't, I'm perfectly capable of looking after a child on my own——'

'And you'd want that?' His thick brows drew together as he regarded her as though she weren't quite sane.

'No,' she breathed. 'But in the circumstances——'

'Circumstances be damned!' Surprisingly easily, aided by his stick, he got to his feet. 'If we've created a child——' roughly he gripped her arm again ' —I want to be part of its life! And, however you feel about me, you're not leaving this house until I know!'

Oh, heaven! He'd be that cruel? There was desperation in her voice as she uttered, 'I've got a right to go whenever and wherever I please!'

'Do that,' he said, 'and I'll find you!' Anger had replaced the bleak look of a few moments ago.

'Even though you might have found someone else?'

She couldn't help it. Her lacerated emotions brought the accusation spilling out of her and her heart felt as if it was being wrung when, after the briefest hesitancy, he acknowledged with a hard expansion of his chest, 'Even though I might have found someone else.'

Pain speared her and she tried to tug out of his grasp, fighting both grief and that unrelenting strength as he restrained her.

'Sasha . . .' his voice was low and husky '. . . give us this much at least. Stay until you know—one way or the other. That's all I'm asking.'

If she hadn't known better she might have said there was suffering of some kind in his face—a suffering every bit as deep as hers. But, of course, she was only imagining things, she thought, those shadows darkening the skin under his eyes caused by the clouds that were suddenly blocking out the sun, and she nodded, too choked to speak. Let him believe that if he wanted to. How could she bear the agony of staying? The knowledge that from now until the day she left another woman would be waiting to take her place?

But if she went to New York and she *was* pregnant— what then? a little reasoning voice inside her asked. Rex, as the child's father, would have a right to know. And equally that child would have every right to a father's love and support. She couldn't deny either of them that, no matter how painful it was for her not to pack up and leave right away. And it would probably only be a matter of days before she knew . . .

'You're cold. For heaven's sake! Go back inside!'

Flinching from the sudden, solicitous arm around her shoulders, hastily Sasha pulled away, chilled to the bone, not from anything physical, but from the sudden possibility presenting itself that if she *were* pregnant he might insist on marrying her after all. And if he did, would she be strong enough to refuse him? Or would she—for his child's sake—accept? Because if she did, could she face the eternal knowledge, the pain—perhaps even his resentment—that he'd really wanted someone else?

That, she thought, with a heart like lead as she moved over the patio into the garden room, was a bridge she would have to cross when she eventually came to it.

CHAPTER TEN

DETERMINEDLY, knowing it was now or never, Sasha steeled herself to go downstairs and give Rex the news.

She knew it now—the result they had both been waiting for. In fact, she had known for a few hours, but had put off actually telling him.

Now, as she came into his study, saw his dark head bowed over the desk, anguish clutched at her stomach. How could she bear it? Face the inevitability of feelings he would be unable to hide when she told him?

'Sasha?' Those dark, discerning eyes were probing hers as though they could see her inner turmoil, but for her own sake she tried to look icily contained, determined to get it over with.

'I thought you'd want to know...'

Maybe it was her hesitation that made those fingers around his pen tauten like steel, but the same rigidity was mirrored in his face as he prompted quickly, 'Yes?'

He knew why she had come, the tension she saw in his face making her swallow to ease the dryness in her throat.

'I'm not pregnant,' she breathed, her voice sounding thin and strangled because suddenly she was battling not to cry. Perhaps it was because during the past few days she'd entertained the craziest hope that she might be, knowing that then at least she would always have a link with him. And for the same reason she hadn't wanted to tell him immediately that she wasn't, because now that link had been well and truly severed.

'I see.' If he was relieved, he was doing a good job of keeping it from showing. 'And now you're going home?'

Why did he make it sound as though she had any say in the matter? Wasn't it he who had wanted to call the engagement off?

'Yes.' There was a weary slump to her shoulders beneath her casual, short-sleeved blouse. 'I've already booked a flight for tomorrow.'

He essayed a thin, humourless smile. 'You didn't waste much time.'

What did he expect her to do? Wait around and watch while another woman stepped into her shoes?

Doing her utmost to conceal the raw anguish inside her, she murmured, 'There didn't seem much point.'

'No,' he averred, and he seemed to need the deepest of breaths to say it. 'What time are you leaving so I can arrange to take you——?'

'That won't be necessary,' she cut in. 'I've arranged to drive myself and then for an auto dealer to come and pick up my car from the airport. I thought it would save you the time and trouble of disposing of it after I've gone.'

And please don't look at me like that! her heart was suddenly screaming, because his gaze was holding hers with a strangely heart-twisting intensity and she could feel her self-possession threatening to crumble.

'You've thought of everything, haven't you?' His tone was clipped, almost cynical. 'Well, that's very considerate of you—but I'm afraid *I* consider it necessary, Sasha. Drive your own car if you will, but you aren't stepping on that plane without my being there. Now what time is your flight?'

She didn't want to tell him. She didn't think she'd be able to cope with saying goodbye to him in a crowded airport without breaking down. But if she didn't, all he would have to do would be to check the flight reservation to find out, and so reluctantly she told him.

'Thank you,' he said incisively as though she'd been withholding something to which he had every right. Didn't he realise what it would cost her tomorrow having him there? she agonised, about to protest just as the telephone rang on his desk.

He picked it up, snapping a response into the mouthpiece while indicating with a hand for Sasha to stay.

What was the point, though? she sighed, hearing his rasped, 'What now? Can't it wait?' catching the frustration in those deep tones when it obviously couldn't and she was granted a merciful escape.

There wasn't anything left to say between them, so why was he trying to prolong it? As he'd said, sex was all it had been—at least on his part, anyway, she thought achingly, and the sooner she was on that plane home the better. Only later, though, after Rex had gone out and she was folding her clothes neatly into her suitcase, did she silently admit that she was only fooling herself. She didn't want to leave him. It would be like leaving a vital part of herself behind, because without him she would never be able to function in quite the same way again.

But she'd go on living. Bravely she squared her shoulders as she emptied the gaping drawers. People did, she thought. And she'd loved and lost before, but she had come through it. And it was hardly as tragic as last time, was it? she tried to ease the depth of her loss by reasoning, even if it felt like it—even if she felt as though she was dying inside herself. It was just that this time the man she loved quite simply preferred someone else . . .

She barely slept that night. Someone tapped softly on her door around midnight and she knew from those laboured footsteps that it was Rex, but she pretended to be asleep. Talking to him wouldn't have made things any easier, she thought abjectly, tossing and turning in the huge four-poster bed. That farewell conversation with Sheila had been painful enough when the woman, freshly informed by Rex that the engagement was off, had come up to express her regrets.

'I must confess I was uneasy about the two of you getting engaged at first,' she had admitted, sitting there beside Sasha on the bed. 'But only because it was so sudden—because I was naturally concerned for Rex—but now . . . well, I don't know what to say.' It was clear she was thoroughly shaken by the news. 'All couples have teething problems,' she'd gone on to advise, concerned. 'And Rex hasn't actually enlarged beyond the fact that it was by mutual agreement— and it's your business, I know—but don't you think that this trip to New York . . . some time apart perhaps might help to resolve whatever's wrong?'

Sheila had known the answer just by looking at her, Sasha realised. Her hopelessness had been reflected in her face. And Rosalind Beckington could scarcely have been termed a teething problem! she thought bitterly, waking for the umpteenth time to a ray of dim light sifting through a chink in the heavy curtains.

She glanced at her clock. It was hours yet until her flight. Hours until the moment she said goodbye to Rex at the airport, and then, as if nothing had happened, stepped on to the plane and out of his life for good. How could he expect her to? Be that insensitive? she agonised, stifling a sob. Didn't he realise that every second spent in that air terminal with him would be like an hour spent on the rack?

Oh, God! She wouldn't cry! she thought as emotion threatened to engulf her. She'd promised herself she'd never let him see her with red and puffy eyes. If she did, he'd know then how much she loved him, and how his decision to end their relationship was tearing her apart. And the only way to avoid that, she thought, as the scalding tears triumphed and squeezed out from beneath her lids, was to go now! Simply leave him a note and get away before he was up. That way she would be spared the torture of final goodbyes, and he would have to respect her wishes.

Consequently, within twenty minutes she was up and dressed and then, slipping her ring off and placing it on top of the sealed envelope on her dressing-table, she stole quietly out of the house.

The sun was just rising over the wheatfields as she drove through the deserted Suffolk lanes, and, pulling down the visor, she wound her window down fully, needing the revitalising fresh air for the lengthy drive ahead.

The loss of a night's sleep wasn't recommended before a three-thousand-mile journey! she thought, sighing, because she'd never been able to sleep on a plane. Nor was it helping her concentration either! she berated herself, startled, when on the slope of a junction the sudden blast of a horn had her yanking on her hand-brake, realising she'd been in danger of rolling back into a solitary milk-float behind.

Pulling away, she could see the river, sparkling in the distance, a twisting silver strand cutting its way through the fields. She had left the Halt without a glance back, afraid she would have broken down completely if she had. Now, though, each mile that took her further from it was like a cruel hand wringing her heart.

She wasn't only leaving Rex. She was leaving this beautiful country as well. A country she would probably never see again, she thought with tears stinging her eyes. At least, not until enough years had passed to have eased the pain she was feeling now...

Trying to shake off emotion, she steered the Mini down towards the river. She knew she was torturing herself, but she had to have one last look.

Parking on the grassy bank, she urged herself out of the car, leaving her jacket on top of her case on the back seat in a deliberate attempt to feel the punishing freshness of the morning, needing to restore her composure before driving on.

Across the water, a field of brown cows sat chewing peacefully in the sun. Sheep bleated near the outbuildings of a distant farm, and closer to hand a skylark's light notes trilled incessantly somewhere overhead.

Why couldn't things have been different? she reflected painfully, unconsciously rubbing her bare arms. That night he had proposed had been the happiest of her life, and then Rosalind Beckington had to come back. And here she was, leaving everything she'd grown to love. England. This countryside. Rex.

Tears trembled on her lower lids, her eyes closing to try and repress them. Oh, God, Rex . . .

'Hey, look out!'

A shout brought her head round to see an early dog-walker running towards her, but he was gesticulating at something beyond her and she whirled round, gasping in horror.

Her Mini was in motion, and heading straight towards the river!

Frantically, Sasha darted after it, followed by the man and his now gleefully barking dog. But the car was moving too fast even to endeavour to stop it and, helplessly, Sasha watched as it plunged off the bank into the water.

'Oh, no!' Horrified, she saw the little blue bonnet submerge beneath the surface, and with a whispered, 'My things!' she was kicking off her shoes and wading in, gasping from the shock of the cold river.

A couple of feet from the bank she stopped. It was pointless trying to wade out any further. All she was doing was getting her jeans wet, she thought despairingly. The water was more than halfway up the Mini's doors anyway and was pouring in through the window she had opened earlier.

'I'll get the police.' The dog-walker's words barely registered as she waded in her uncomfortably wet jeans back to the bank. 'I'll flag down the next car that comes along.'

And that must have been how they managed to arrive so swiftly, Sasha realised afterwards, sipping hot chocolate in the police station with a rug around her shoulders, sitting in a pair of borrowed baggy trousers because a policewoman had taken her jeans away to be dried.

'You say you were staying with a friend?'

From behind the desk, a young officer was diligently taking down her particulars, and Sasha nodded, chewing on her bottom lip.

'Then won't this friend——?'

'No!' The word was strung with panic. She didn't want Rex involved! It had been hard enough leaving him in the manner she'd left this morning. She couldn't face him again—especially in the state she was in now. She was desperate that he shouldn't know. 'If you could just get a call through to the American embassy...'

'Someone's taking care of that. The line's probably busy.' The young man glanced up from his notes at a colleague who had just strode in behind him and as the second man looked her way Sasha's heart sank. He was one of the officers who had called at the Halt the day her car had been broken into—and he'd recognised her, she realised, as he exchanged a few quiet words with the younger man.

'A bit unfortunate, isn't it, Miss...' he glanced down at the first officer's report '...Morgan...losing everything twice?'

She saw the first officer battling with a smile, feeling near to despair herself. As if she didn't have enough problems without *this* happening, she thought frustratedly as the younger man excused himself and left the desk. It was like some nightmare that at any second she might wake up from, except that she knew she was fully awake.

And how long she sat there she wasn't sure, watching people come and go, but, glancing up suddenly, with a surge of conflicting emotions she was uttering a startled, 'Rex!'

'What on earth have you been up to?' he rasped.

She couldn't decide what the ruling emotion was on that strong face as he limped, stick-assisted, towards her. His anger was evident, but was it relief she saw behind that? she wondered with a self-destructive little ray of hope. 'What the devil was I supposed to think? First I find you gone—with only the consideration of a polite little note by way of explanation—and the next thing I know, the police are ringing me to tell me you've put your car into the river! Didn't you think I wouldn't be worried enough without thinking you'd been trying to drown yourself as well?'

'I wasn't trying to drown myself!' she snapped, wondering if he was just angry or really as worried as he seemed. He certainly looked as though he'd left in a rush. Tieless, his shirt was still open at the neck beneath his light suit jacket as though he'd been in the act of dressing when he'd got the call. 'Something was wrong with the hand-brake,' she went on, relieved—in spite of everything—that he was there. 'I got out for some air and the next thing I knew, the car was running down the bank!'

Neither of them was fully aware of the senior police officer behind the desk and Sasha's jaw tightened defiantly as those proud nostrils dilated with anger.

'You had no business running off like that without a word to anyone that you were going!'

'I had *every* business!' The rug slid from her shoulders as his audacity brought her to her feet. 'I told you yesterday that I could manage on my own but you wouldn't listen!'

'No?' One eyebrow climbed, his mouth suddenly twitching at the hideously oversized trousers, bunched

and belted at the waist, making Sasha colour from
the foolishness of her statement. She'd managed perfectly well—by ending up with her car in the river!

'I understand everything's underwater. Passport.
Air ticket. Clothes.'

Did he have to rub it in? she thought, adding
somewhat poignantly, 'You forgot the sketches,' because everything she'd painted since she had been in
England had been in that car. Well, almost everything, anyway, she thought, infinitely relieved that Rex
had posted her *Corn Dolly* for her several days ago
and that it was now safely on its way to her New York
publisher.

'In that case, it's just as well you won't be going
home today,' he drawled, and she wondered how he
could be saying things like this, hurting her so much
when she was already hurting excruciatingly—simply
having him there. 'If you'll excuse the unfortunate
choice of pun, you seem to be in exactly the same
boat as before,' he was commenting drily. And as she
opened her mouth to make some angry retort, 'Why
don't you admit it, darling . . .' his voice was suddenly
soft, devoid of either anger or amusement '. . . you're
a walking disaster—totally out of control without me?'

Coming as it did, so unexpectedly, the endearment
alone was enough to send traitorous impulses leaping
through her, even without the implication of his
remark, which now had her anger fleeing on a wave
of aching response.

Pain surfaced in her eyes and futilely she ques-
tioned his. They were unfathomable beyond that
mesmeric potency that seemed to be stripping her to
the soul. And then she heard the police officer give
an intervening cough behind them, say to Rex, 'Why

don't you take her in there, sir? It'll be nice and private—and I'll see you're not disturbed. By the way, it's good to see you back on your feet.'

With a brief word of thanks, Rex was hustling Sasha towards the room the man had indicated, leaning against the door he closed behind them, his body obstructing any escape.

'Oh, I see! You've even got the police on your side now!' The gibe was a front, the few seconds it had taken to get from the outer room to this one with its plain table and chairs and plain walls a blessed lapse for her to bring her raging emotions under control.

'Not the police—just cold, calculated reasoning,' he said, folding his arms, looking every bit the hard interrogator—the man who would wrest the truth from his captive whatever the cost. 'I might be wrong, but if you're so indifferent to me why didn't you have the courage of your convictions and allow me to see you to the airport? I freed you from our commitment without any animosity. So why would you run away from our last few hours together if our engagement had meant so little to you? Unless, of course, it was going to hurt too much to say goodbye.'

Oh, God! He was too clever! She'd intended to leave without him knowing so that he wouldn't realise the truth, and now that very action had served to show him just how much in love with him she was!

'You were right.' She was striving for bored indifference. 'You're wrong!' she snapped, making a vain attempt to open the door. Vain because those hard, lean hips were suddenly and effectively blocking the handle, and Sasha pulled back from the intimate contact as though it had the power of a piranha.

'Am I?' Tossing his stick aside, he was reaching for her, ignoring her protests as he pulled her against him. 'Look me in the eyes and say that. Tell me I'm wrong now.'

She couldn't, because the needs of her heart and body were gaining sway over the hollow objections of her mind, the traitorous ecstasy of being in his arms again crushing all her powers of resistance.

'No,' he said firmly, denying himself satisfaction of the lips unwittingly upturned to his, though she could feel his chest expanding against hers with the effort. 'I want you to tell me that it isn't just physical. I want you to tell me I'm right.'

'Why?' She lowered her lids to hide the wounded defeat she was feeling, watching a pulse throb beneath the dark strength of his throat. 'So you can have two strings to your bow?'

Hard puzzlement etched his features as he held her away, studying the bitter accusation in hers. 'What the devil is that supposed to mean?'

'Heavens, Rex!' It came out on a mirthless little chuckle. 'You really know how to lay it on! I opened the letter—remember?'

'The letter?'

He was still managing to look baffled, only allowing comprehension to show through just before she uttered, 'Rosalind Beckington.' And then he laughed. And he was still laughing! she realised bitterly, feeling his grip tightening when she tried to pull away.

'Are you accusing me of two-timing you?' he quizzed with a good show of disbelief. And when she didn't answer, 'Oh, I'll admit Rosalind played an important part in my life——'

'Don't I know it!' she breathed sarcastically.

'News certainly travels!' He stared down into her strained, flushed features, his mouth a cynical curve. 'Well, if you know about Rosalind and me you'll have the good sense to realise that it's finished. And if you're imagining I didn't mention that letter because I wanted to carry on some passionate, clandestine affair with an ex-girlfriend you're wrong! I thought it best forgotten—beyond mentioning. I'd already made a commitment to you. I would have hoped that would have counted with you for something!'

'Why?' She jerked her head accusingly upwards. 'When you could forget about it the instant you found yourself alone with her in your office?'

His eyes narrowed to chips of slate and it was like her own blood seeping out of her when she saw Rex's drain from his face. 'How,' he said slowly, 'did you know about that?'

'We had a date that evening—remember?' Her tone held a frosty bitterness and numbly she saw the shock—the clarity dawning in his eyes. 'Contrary to what you thought,' she went on with a small sob in her voice, 'I *did* keep it. I came up to your office a bit earlier than we'd arranged but you were otherwise *engaged*! And don't try telling me she means nothing to you because I heard you admit it yourself! And it didn't just stop at conversation, did it?' she threw at him, the torture of remembering making itself evident now, but she didn't care any more. 'Tell me, Rex.' Her words were bitter—a taunt. 'Does she kiss as well as I do?'

'No.'

No? Oh, heaven! What was he saying? How could he be so calm, so... heartless when his phlegmatic attitude was tearing her to shreds?

'You mean... you're not even trying to deny you kissed her?' she murmured in a small, wounded voice. How could he stand there looking so unrepentant? In fact, worse than that, practically amused!

'I'm not denying that I let her kiss *me*.'

'Oh, come on!' She wasn't buying that! 'From where I was standing you didn't seem to be objecting. You could have prevented it if you'd wanted to, but you didn't want to, did you? I'm sure a woman couldn't kiss *you* unless you wanted her to, so you must have let it happen.'

'Yes.'

'Why?' she breathed, his truthfulness piercing her like the cruellest blade, and in answer she saw his mouth suddenly harden.

'Because she was so darn persistent. So convinced we still had what was there before, and no amount of argument would make her see that it wasn't the case. I *welcomed* her kiss—to show her just how immune I was. No, not immune. That's too strong a word. That implies a conscious need on my part to resist her. Indifferent would be the best way to describe my feelings towards her—and from my lack of response to that kiss she realised it. Obviously you didn't stick around or you'd probably have collided with her. She stormed out of my office like the proverbial woman scorned. And you...' his tone and expression had softened, and gently his hands came to rest on her shoulders '...you left—thinking I was in love with her? Wandering off for hours in the pouring rain.

Is that why you wanted me to think you were with Gavin?'

The emotion flooding through her was so intense that she could only nod, feeling the caress of his hands on her shoulders like a soothing balm.

'You and your imagination.' His wry smile—that gentle reproof—made her heart flip. 'You nearly ruined your life before through imagining things,' he rebuked softly, reminding her of all the heart-searching guilt—the unnecessary pain—she had suffered because of Ben. 'You imagined I was deceiving you—could hurt you that much? And there *I* was thinking you were simply regretting having got engaged, and were feeling too sorry for me to break it off.'

'You what?' Incredulity lit her eyes from his startling admission. 'Why did you think that?'

He shrugged. 'Oh, I don't know.' His fingers were threading through the shining strands of her hair, sending little shivers of pleasure down her spine. 'You seemed so...restless. Always doing things—active things—and with Gavin. Enjoying a lifestyle I thought I'd never be able to give you. I thought I was being unfair to you—tying you down.'

'Now who's been imagining things?' she chided smilingly, slipping her arms eagerly around his neck.

And understood when he pulled a wry face and said, 'Can you blame me? I wasn't a very exciting prospect for the future—being stuck in that darn chair!'

With a deep sigh of contentment, she laid her head against his shoulder. 'I wasn't looking for excitement,' she murmured, amazed to realise the depths of his own insecurities. 'I said yes because...'

'Yes?' he prompted, tilting her chin with a fore-finger so that she was forced to look into his face.

'Because I love you,' she whispered, deciding to end any further misunderstandings between them now.

'And did you think I didn't feel the same way about *you*? Why the hell do you think I asked you to marry me in the first place, you crazy little idiot? Did you imagine I made a habit of proposing to any little waif I happened to take into my house? And after only a few weeks at that? It was only my legs that had been paralysed—not my brain! And the only reason I managed to get out of that chair that night,' he went on with a sudden hoarseness to his voice, 'was because I was so desperate not to lose you. What more could any man do, my love, to show a woman how much he cares?'

'I didn't know.' She couldn't say any more because her heart was too full, her happiness immeasurable as he crushed her against the hard wall of his chest.

'When you told me you weren't pregnant, it was like losing my last chance of keeping you with me,' he said with a raw, suppressed emotion. 'I had to do something—that's why I was so adamant about seeing you to the airport—to do my darnedest to try and make you change your mind. Up until then I'd been praying—yes, *praying*——' he gave a shuddering laugh as though it was somehow alien to him '—that you'd come and tell me that we'd created another little life that night. I'd pictured a replica of you. Someone I could bounce on my knee. Somehow I couldn't en-visage anything but the three of us together. A family. You as my wife...'

His embrace slackened so that he could take some-thing out of his trouser pocket. The box with her ring inside! she noticed with a little gasp of joy. 'Let's start again,' he advised softly, lifting her hand and slipping it back on to her finger, smiling down at the radiant emotion in her eyes. 'And I'm sorry to know you weren't looking for excitement,' he murmured, with a pulse-quickening glimmer in his, 'because I'm planning just about as much as you can handle.'

A delicious little tingle ran down her spine and then his mouth was covering hers at last, his kiss bringing her straining towards him, desire fuelling desire.

'I'll bet no one's ever done this in here before,' he whispered against her lips, the incongruity of their surroundings with the unflatteringly masculine trousers she was wearing making her giggle, just as someone knocked on the door.

'The young lady's call to the embassy,' the officer who had recognised her announced when Rex opened it.

Looking at Sasha, he grimaced. 'Tell them it was a false alarm,' he instructed the other man drily. 'And if you aren't planning to lock her up, Officer, I'll be making myself responsible for her future behaviour by taking her home with me.'

'No, we won't be pressing charges, sir.' The policeman winked at Sasha, joining in the joke. 'Not if she returns the trousers to this station within seven days.'

'Did you *have* to say that?' Sasha laughed, pink-cheeked, when the other man returned to his business. 'You seem to have forgotten the seriousness of the situation. I'm without everything! My car. All my clothes. My money! And, engaged or not, I don't like feeling——'

'Indebted?' Shrugging out of his jacket, he placed it around her shoulders. His scent clung to it as Sasha drew it around her, stirring the memory of the first time he had done that, the day she had come down in that balloon. 'I forgot how fiercely independent you are,' he said wryly, 'but don't worry—we'll get your things fished out of that river. I'm sure there'll be something there worth salvaging! In the meantime, if you insist on earning your keep...' Retrieving his stick, smilingly he opened the door for her. 'I've always wanted a mural in the master bedroom. When Clem's got us home, I'll take you up and show you just what ideas I've got in mind.'

A sensually induced little shiver tingled down Sasha's spine. 'Of an artistic nature, sir?' she queried laughingly, her arm going automatically around his waist.

With a nod at the policeman standing grinning at them behind the desk, Rex drew her close as they walked together out to the car, uttering in laughing response, 'Oh, definitely!'

Accept 4 FREE Romances and 2 FREE gifts

FROM READER SERVICE

Here's an irresistible invitation from Mills & Boon. Please accept our offer of 4 FREE Romances, a CUDDLY TEDDY and a special MYSTERY GIFT! Then, if you choose, go on to enjoy 6 captivating Romances every month for just £1.90 each, postage and packing FREE. Plus our FREE Newsletter with author news, competitions and much more.

Send the coupon below to:
Mills & Boon Reader Service,
FREEPOST, PO Box 236,
Croydon, Surrey CR9 9EL.

- - - - - - - **NO STAMP REQUIRED** - - - - - - -

Yes! Please rush me 4 FREE Romances and 2 FREE gifts! Please also reserve me a Reader Service subscription. If I decide to subscribe I can look forward to receiving 6 brand new Romances for just £11.40 each month, post and packing FREE. If I decide not to subscribe I shall write to you within 10 days - I can keep the free books and gifts whatever I choose. I may cancel or suspend my subscription at any time. I am over 18 years of age.

Ms/Mrs/Miss/Mr _____ EP70R

Address _____

_____

Postcode _____ Signature _____

mps MAILING PREFERENCE SERVICE